The gunner sprinted to the car, shouting orders to the driver

"There's nothing I like better than putting drug scum out of business!" Jack Grimaldi leaned forward in his seat and steered the JetRanger into the pull of gravity, swooping down on the gesticulating figure. Quinones's face was a study in terror as he spotted the attacking helicopter.

"I'll give you a target in three, two, one!" Grimaldi shouted, then rotated the chopper, presenting the car to Bolan, who grabbed the MM-1 and triggered two 40 mm HE projectiles toward the vehicle.

The pilot twisted the JetRanger at the last moment to avoid clipping the car, and the grenades skimmed the top of the roof, skittering across to explode harmlessly on the ground fifteen feet away.

"Damn."

"Don't worry about it," the Executioner assured him. "They're fish in a barrel. Get us overhead."

D0976496

MACK BOLAN ®
The Executioner

DON PENDLETON'S

THE EXECUTIONER®

HOSTILE PROXIMITY

A GOLD EAGLE BOOK FROM

WORLDWIDE®

TORONTO • NEW YORK • LONDON
AMSTERDAM • PARIS • SYDNEY • HAMBURG
STOCKHOLM • ATHENS • TOKYO • MILAN
MADRID • WARSAW • BUDAPEST • AUCKLAND

First edition November 1998
ISBN 0-373-64239-3

Special thanks and acknowledgment to
Tim Somheil for his contribution to this work.

HOSTILE PROXIMITY

Printed in U.S.A.

Nothing can excuse a general who takes advantage of the knowledge of his country to deliver up her frontiers and her towns to foreigners. This is a crime reprobated by every principle of religion, morality, and honor.

—Napoleon I
Maxims of War, 1831

When power is up for grabs, morality and honor are rare, rare commodities.

—Mack Bolan

THE
MACK BOLAN®
LEGEND

Nothing less than a war could have fashioned the destiny of the man called Mack Bolan. Bolan earned the Executioner title in the jungle hell of Vietnam.

But this soldier also wore another name—Sergeant Mercy. He was so tagged because of the compassion he showed to wounded comrades-in-arms and Vietnamese civilians.

Mack Bolan's second tour of duty ended prematurely when he was given emergency leave to return home and bury his family, victims of the Mob. Then he declared a one-man war against the Mafia.

He confronted the Families head-on from coast to coast, and soon a hope of victory began to appear. But Bolan had broken society's every rule. That same society started gunning for this elusive warrior—to no avail.

So Bolan was offered amnesty to work within the system against terrorism. This time, as an employee of Uncle Sam, Bolan became Colonel John Phoenix. With a command center at Stony Man Farm in Virginia, he and his new allies—Able Team and Phoenix Force—waged relentless war on a new adversary: the KGB.

But when his one true love, April Rose, died at the hands of the Soviet terror machine, Bolan severed all ties with Establishment authority.

Now, after a lengthy lone-wolf struggle and much soul-searching, the Executioner has agreed to enter an "arm's-length" alliance with his government once more, reserving the right to pursue personal missions in his Everlasting War.

12:03 a.m.

The Sea Stallion decelerated to fifty miles per hour and swept in an arc toward the surface of the Caribbean, which gleamed like the edge of a glimmering black diamond in the night. The pilot used one hand to press the headphone to his ear as he leveled the U.S. Navy helicopter less than twenty feet above the water.

"What's up?" his passenger asked. The man behind the pilot wore a black wet suit. With his dark hair and hooded eyes, he had the appearance of a malevolent wraith turned human, the kind of man nobody would want to meet in a dark alley.

The pilot, on the other hand, had pleasant, narrow, features. He listened to the headphone for a moment longer, then said over the roar of the engines, "Company's coming!"

"DAAFAR?"

The pilot nodded. "Yeah. Reconnaissance spotted an MiG-29—it's gotta be Cuban."

"ETA?"

"Two minutes."

"Then I'm getting out early."

"You'll have a long boat ride ahead of you."

"It can't be helped."

The pilot looked thoughtful for a second, trying to come up with an alternative plan that would be more advantageous to his partner. Then he nodded again. "You're right—get out here!"

The passenger yanked on a handle and the side of the Sea Stallion slid open, revealing the pitch-black Caribbean water. The pilot suddenly slowed the craft, but even before it stopped the other man had shoved out the raft package, which began to inflate during its descent. Another package followed, containing a specially designed motor to propel the raft. It hit the water and bobbed instantly to the surface.

"Thanks for the lift, Jack," the man in black said with a quick wave.

"Raise some hell!"

"Never," the dark man said, and stepped into open space.

Mack Bolan, a.k.a. the Executioner, plummeted to the black tropical water and felt it envelop him with a flurry of bubbles. When he rose to the top, the Sea Stallion was already ascending into the empty night.

It wasn't empty for long.

JACK GRIMALDI WAS ace pilot for Stony Man Farm, home of the most top-secret and effective strike forces in the U.S. The man he had just dumped unceremoniously into the ocean in the middle of nowhere was the namesake of the Farm. Grimaldi didn't often have doubts about Bolan's safety.

But right now there was a Russian-built, Cuban air force MiG coming to check out the situation. There'd be problems if they spotted Bolan's small life raft.

That wasn't going to happen. Grimaldi fed thrust to the Sea Stallion and the helo screeched into the sky, sweeping northward, until he leveled it off at one thousand feet and sped north, accelerating more than eighty miles per hour.

The radioman at Guantánamo gave him a proximity warning, and Grimaldi looked up as an MiG-29 Fulcrum scorched the night sky a mile above him. Grimaldi smiled and waved, chuckling. He'd put plenty of space between himself and Bolan. The odds of the Cubans tracking the soldier now were infinitesimal.

Bolan was safe.

Grimaldi grimaced. *Safe* was not really a good choice of words.

There was nothing safe about the Executioner.

BOLAN FLOPPED into the raft and hauled the bobbing engine after him, unpacking it. He heard the distant roar of the MiG and watched it streak across the sky above him. In a minute the Sea Stallion and the MiG had both disappeared, and the night was quiet save for the gentle heaving of the Caribbean.

He attached the electric engine to the raft, started it, brought it to high revs and started skimming through the peaceful sea. He had a long trip ahead of him—longer than planned, due to the unexpectedly quick arrival of the Cubans.

But the night was young. A lot could be accomplished before dawn.

3:43 a.m.

THE BOAT WAS a thirty-four-foot flying bridge cruiser, a pleasure craft for those who could afford such luxuries or for commercial outfits selling day-trips to tourists. It didn't belong in these waters. There weren't many Cubans who could afford one, and there were no tourist ports in the area. If the cruiser had drifted in from international waters, its occupants were in a lot of danger.

But Bolan knew there were no innocents aboard.

His first sight of an onboard guard wielding an AK-74 autorifle had convinced him of that.

Not many vacationers in the Caribbean felt the need to carry automatic weapons.

The Executioner switched off the electric motor and paddled in from the rear of the cruiser, where he wasn't likely to be spotted. But there were no guarantees, and he remained alert every second, ready to draw the large handgun holstered under his shoulder at a moment's notice.

His luck held, and soon he had tied the raft to the small boarding deck at the rear of the cruiser and stepped on board.

He heard the low rumble of quiet voices, muffled by the gentle lapping of the ocean against the sides of the boat.

It was so quiet, in fact, that Bolan knew even the cough of a silenced, subsonic round from his drawn gun would be perfectly audible throughout the craft.

He had to move with utmost caution.

Taking the single stair down, he placed his ear against the door at the bottom and listened. The voices within were speaking Russian, idle conversation about a long wait. Something about trust. Bolan knew enough Russian to understand that the two men inside were passing time, waiting. But waiting for what?

He detected a faint hum, like a bee buzzing from the other side of the room, but growing closer, and he knew another boat was coming. A rendezvous was about to take place. When it did, many of his questions would be answered.

He quickly made his way back up and to the rear of the cruiser, replacing the handgun in a waterproof pack and, drawing a stiletto from his calf sheath, he stabbed the raft repeatedly, reducing it to scrap rubber that the electric motor dragged bubbling into the ocean. So much for his escape route—but he couldn't have the boat sitting there when the newcomers tried to dock.

The buzz of the motor was getting louder, and the guard onboard gave a call. Again it was in Russian, but it was clearly meant to inform the men in the cabin of the approaching vessel. Bolan slid into the Caribbean, the dark water covering all but the top of his head. Then he edged through the water, around the side of the craft, away from where the approaching boat would stop.

And he waited.

BOLAN HAD STARTED on this trail just twenty-four hours earlier in Cap Haitien, a major Haitian port, where he had been tracking a massive shipment of cocaine worth millions on the streets of the U.S., or wherever it was headed. The product belonged to a young, aggressive cartel that looked like it was on the fast track to international narcotics stardom. The man in charge was Manny Quinones, who had spent years as a minor player in the Cali cartel. He was now taking his experience and striking out on his own. A number of ex-Cali enforcers and management had gone with him. Their little entrepreneurial venture was just starting to hit the big time. If the shipment they were shuttling through Haiti was any indication, they were about to make some major sales. With the kind of capital they would be bringing in, Quinones would have every right to call himself one of the major players in international narcotics supply.

Bolan was of the opinion that another major player wasn't needed and planned to do some serious damage to the new cartel's profit margins.

Then things got strange. In Cap Haitien, Bolan found the drugs had been transferred to a boat called the *Ocean Missed*. The men guarding the vessel had Russian accents—in fact they spoke Russian when they thought no one else was listening.

Bolan took some surveillance photos and faxed them to Aaron Kurtzman at Stony Man Farm, who identified one of the men on board as Major Alex Sablin of the former Soviet KGB. He had been part of the attempted coup d'état against Boris Yeltsin in the early 1990s and, after its failure, had disappeared. It had been assumed he had fled Russia forever with a group of supporters.

So what was he doing smuggling drugs in the tropics?

Bolan decided to let the *Ocean Missed* go on its way. Maybe he could learn what was going down.

He had never thought he would end up in Cuban waters.

THE OTHER VESSEL SLOWED as it neared the stern of the cruiser, and Bolan heard a shout in Spanish that quickly turned to English.

"Is Sablin there?"

"Yes? I am Major Alex Sablin. Where is General Solas?"

"One moment."

Solas, Bolan thought, didn't sound like a Russian name.

"I am Solas." Bolan felt the thump of a plank placed between the two vessels, and the man stepped across it. "It is good to meet you finally."

That accent was Cuban, which could only mean Solas was with the Cuban navy or another armed forces division.

"We heard trouble on the radio earlier," Sablin said.

"No trouble," Solas answered. "Just an American helicopter out of Guantánamo going off course, nosing around. They do it all the time. And there's not much we can do about it if they stay outside our three-mile perimeter. He didn't get into Cuban airspace, and we sent a jet to shoo him away. No problem."

"Good. How are things proceeding?"

Suddenly the voices were gone. Solas and Sablin had moved inside the cabin. All Bolan could hear was the idle chatter of the Russian and the Cuban crews.

That chatter informed Bolan that they were starting the process of transferring their cargo into the Cuban navy vessel.

So the drugs were going to Cuba, under the guard of a Cuban navy general who was somehow in league with an ex-KGB major.

Bolan knew he was a long way from having all the pieces, but the puzzle that was starting to take form made a startling picture, indeed.

"SO TELL ME, from your heart what the feeling is among the top navy brass, General. How is this plan being received?"

"Good."

"But?" Sablin asked.

"But, Comrade, I am moving very slowly. I have not brought too many men into my confidence as of yet. You know that I must be careful to relay these plans only to those who I am sure will buy into them."

"I understand that."

"Even the men whom I know are Marxists at their core can

be doubtful that a new revolution is called for. It can be a slow process. And if I misjudge even one man the consequences could be disastrous. There has already been one near miss.''

"What do you mean by a 'near miss'?" Sablin asked, handing Solas a glass of vodka.

"One of my most trusted captains," Solas said. He sipped his drink and waved the glass, threatening to spill his liquor on the carpet. "I took him into my confidence. I thought he would be very much for joining us. He was one of the last people I would have thought would remain loyal to the old regime in the face of this bold opportunity. But after I told him, he was halfhearted. I was suspicious then, and I had him followed and his phone tapped. He tried to contact Cuban Intelligence. Luckily we have men there, and these men intercepted his call and agreed to meet with him. This man disappeared before he could be of any serious threat.''

Sablin contemplated the story.

"So," Solas added, "you can see why I am moving slowly.''

Sablin nodded. "Yes, of course. But time is moving fast. Soon you will not have the opportunity to examine your recruits so carefully. You will need to take more chances. We must have a network, a web of compatriots in place, and very soon. They will be needed to spread the word once our initiative begins.''

Solas nodded gravely, lifted his glass high, then drank from it.

"To the initiative.''

"To tomorrow's Cuba.''

BOLAN HAD a very definite point of view about narcotics traders.

His feelings didn't change when he discovered the shipment was going to Cuba instead of the United States of America. A life wasted to drug use was a life wasted, no matter where in the world. A dealer ruined people's lives, whether he dealt on the streets of Havana or Miami. In Bolan's eyes the lives of drug smugglers, no matter where they operated, were forfeit.

This case, despite its bizarre turns, was no exception. The Executioner was determined to learn more about what was motivating members of the Cuban navy to bring coke into their country, but he was more determined that the narcotic would never reach its destination.

He had brought a special package intended for the *Ocean Missed,* but he decided to let the Cuban ship have it. In the darkness, swimming slowly and with gentle strokes, he paddled from one vessel to the other.

He clung to the belly of the Cuba ship until he came to a rear ladder, slimy with seaweed. He hoisted himself out of the water long enough to work with the waterproof pack he carried. The brick of plastic-wrapped plastique was more than sufficient to blast a mortal hole into the hull of the Cuban vessel and send it to the bottom with its deadly cargo. He listened for a long minute to gauge the rapidity of the loading process, made a quick estimate and set the detonator time for ten minutes. Wedging the package under the overhanging deck where it wouldn't be discovered, he slipped back into the water.

Swimming with cautious strokes, he reached the open sea between the vessels, where he saw that the cabin door on the *Ocean Missed* was open. Bolan allowed himself to sink lower, so that just his forehead and eyes protruded from the gently swaying ocean. He watched the two men who emerged.

He recognized Sablin, the ex-KGB general, while the other's voice identified him as the Cuban general, Solas.

"Time runs short. We need these funds immediately, General."

"You will have them, Major Sablin."

"This cash is vital to our success. We are depending on it."

"You will have your money!" Solas said. "See you soon, Major."

Bolan submerged and swam to the bow of the *Ocean*

Missed, where he surfaced again cautiously, one fist around the anchor rope. The Cuban vessel was drifting away. Its engines came to life, and it churned the water and headed south.

Solas waved from the deck.

Sablin saluted and strode back among his men. "That fool had better know what he's doing," he muttered in Russian.

"Why does he think he has the resources to sell cocaine profitably?" one of his men asked.

"I don't believe he does," Sablin retorted. "But he's confident enough. We'll see. We need the money."

"What's it marked for?"

Sablin looked at the man as if he were somewhat of a fool. "Men! What else? We have everything we need. Except men."

"Which men?"

Bolan checked his watch. The Cuban ship was two hundred yards away and gaining speed.

Sablin snorted and shrugged. "Resnikoff and Rifkin have a list. They're playing recruiters now."

"Offering money we don't yet have?" the other man asked.

Sablin stopped and leaned against the railing. He watched the Cuban ship and waved at it. "Offering the money Solas will be bringing us."

"What if Solas doesn't bring us all the money he says he will bring?"

Bolan looked at his watch again. He pulled himself up on the anchor rope with one hand and withdrew his Beretta 93-R from the waterproof pack with the other, glancing at the watch one last time.

Four seconds. Three. Two...

"He'll get the money," Sablin declared.

The Cuban ship erupted with a burst of orange-white light and a clap of thunder that shook the peaceful Caribbean. Bolan reached over the side of the ship and dragged himself up, swinging onto the deck and landing on both feet. He swept the open deck before him with his handgun, searching for targets. The deck was clear. He stalked to the rear, where the crew was collecting.

The burning ruin of the Cuban navy vessel was tilting, its back end already submerged, flames stuttering in the salt water and transforming into oily black clouds that funneled into the clear night sky.

A quick count told Bolan his convenient distraction had gathered the entire crew of the *Ocean Missed* in one spot.

"What happened?" Major Sablin asked over the shocked silence.

"I did," Bolan said.

Four people turned on him at once, and one of the armed guards made the fatal mistake of swinging his AK-74 into firing position.

Bolan drilled a tri-burst of 9 mm parabellum rounds into the gunner, taking him out of play.

As the second guard tried to bring his automatic rifle into target acquisition Bolan turned the 93-R on him, triggering a burst that slammed into the gunner's arm and sent his AK fire into the deck of the boat. The Executioner adjusted his aim minutely and sent the next three rounds into the torso of the gunman, punching him to the deck.

There was a flurry of movement as Major Sablin dived to the left and disappeared around the side of the boat, too fast for Bolan, who tried to track him with the 93-R but failed. Then the last man made his move, grabbing for a piece of hardware in his shoulder holster. The Russian's handgun was just clearing leather when the Beretta achieved target acquisition and Bolan stitched him, chest, throat and skull, driving him back into the low wall, which he flipped over before splashing into the water. Seconds later he floated to the surface amid a spreading red stain. Bolan didn't stay to watch.

Instead he jumped around the corner ready to fire—but found only open space. Sablin was gone.

But he wasn't going far.

Bolan crept to the side door and jerked it open, stepping away from the opening to avoid a flurry of bullets that never came. He leaped across the threshold and down the single step into the cabin where the meeting table stood. He snatched open the door to the head and found it empty.

He stopped and listened.

There was a thump—maybe a footstep—then nothing.

He stood in the middle of the cabin, the 93-R held close to his face, and began to turn in a slow circle, waiting. If this was a game of cat and mouse, Bolan knew how to be a very patient cat.

Fifteen seconds. Thirty. There was another sound, faint, like a rustle in the breeze. Then another thump. It was a footstep, no doubt about it this time, and it came from directly overhead.

Sablin had planted himself in the open-air pilot's cabin, where he had a clear view of the entire deck. Bolan couldn't leave the interior without being spotted and targeted instantly.

But the major hadn't covered all contingencies.

Bolan stepped onto the built-in bench and then the table, peering out through the air vent, under a hood on the upper deck. He spotted a pair of feet and ankles standing in the flying bridge.

It would be a difficult shot, but Bolan had the time he needed to set it up carefully. He selected single-fire on the 93-R and pointed the barrel through the narrow opening, targeting one of the ankles as Sablin rotated nervously, trying to cover all directions. He waited until he had a clear shot at the major's Achilles tendon, then fired one round.

The shot was good; he knew it instantly and he jumped from the table and burst through the door even as he heard the sound of the major's body tumbling to the deck. He hopped onto the top deck in time to discover the wounded Russian trying to flip himself onto his stomach and get a firing grip on his Makarov. Bolan targeted the major's hands and fired once again, sending the large handgun plopping into the Caribbean water.

Sablin was shouting in Russian as Bolan climbed to the top deck and stood over him.

"What's going on, Sablin?"

"Who are you, American? CIA? DEA? Tell me!"

"Does it matter? And I get to ask the questions. Why are you selling cocaine to the Cuban navy?"

"Where did you come from? How did you get here? You couldn't have stowed away on this ship."

Bolan knelt and grabbed the injured Russian by the collar and proceeded to drag him to the stern of the boat, where two of Sablin's comrades lay. Another was floating facedown in the ocean several yards away, bouncing like a bobbin. Bolan lifted Sablin, who resisted meekly, and draped him on his stomach over the railing. He grabbed his hair and lifted his head.

"Look what's happening to your friend," Bolan said.

Sablin had no choice but to stare at the corpse, which now flopped sideways in the sea, its grisly white face turning in their direction for a second. Something had removed the corpse's arm and shoulder. A single fin, as pale as the dead man's face, skimmed along the surface of the water and was gone.

Sablin made a whining sound.

"You're next, Major," Bolan said.

"What do you want to know?" Sablin cried.

"Let's say this is a movie and I came in halfway through it. Explain what's happened up to this point."

"I'm KGB!"

"Yes."

"I was in the coup. I left after that. I came to South America. Now I make a living as a drug dealer. There's a bunch of us who do it!"

"Yes?"

"That's all!"

"I think you're leaving out most of the major plot points, Major. Such as why your customers include a Cuban general."

"Who better to smuggle drugs into Cuba? Even generals have no money there!"

"It doesn't make sense, Major. Listen to this dialogue— 'Time runs short. We need these funds immediately.' This is you talking, Major. 'This cash is vital to our success. We're depending on it.' Depending on it for what, Major?''

Sablin said nothing.

"They'll still be hungry, Sablin. They're coming for you next." He felt the Russian trembling. "I suggest you feed me information before I feed you to them."

"*Nyet. Nyet.* There's nothing more I can..." His voice dropped to a whisper. "There's nothing more..."

With a surge of strength Sablin kicked Bolan and swung his free hand at him. The Executioner fell back several steps and leveled the 93-R as the Russian collapsed to the deck and grabbed for a dead man's gun.

"*Nyet,* Comrade," Bolan said.

Sablin, on all fours, looked up, still groping the deck for an AK.

"You'll never make it," Bolan offered.

Sablin's hand found cold metal and froze. "Better to die by a bullet than in the teeth of those monsters."

Bolan couldn't argue. He even admired the man's logic.

Sablin pulled the AK toward him and rose to his knees, flipping the butt of the Kalashnikov into his stomach and reaching for the trigger. He never found it. Bolan triggered the 93-R twice, and black, bloody craters appeared in Sablin's chest. He fell face-forward, the AK under him.

The last of the smoke from the vanished Cuban navy vessel silently dissipated.

The *Ocean Missed* swayed gently in the quiet sea.

The sharks in the Caribbean some four-and-one-third miles northeast of the Cuban port town of Sagua de Tanamo fed very well that night.

2

The *Ocean Missed* nodded quietly in the gentle shallows three hundred yards off the shore of Barry Bay, Jamaica. Bolan sat behind a pair of binoculars watching the land.

Barry Bay was a small town on the north shore of the island nation, just about halfway between Negril and Montego Bay. A small hotel that had existed just east of the village for years, had been changed recently into an all-inclusive resort in a bid to remain competitive with huge vacation destinations nearby. The prices were low, the atmosphere was extremely casual and the beach was clothing-optional, attracting young, wild American singles out for a hedonistic week of abandoned inhibitions.

So Bolan found plenty of interesting sights through the lenses of the Steadyscope.

Not, however, what he'd specifically come looking for.

He allowed the vessel to drift along the shore, never getting too close, and always on the lookout for sandbars and coral. The water was already so shallow he could stand in it without submerging his head.

The village proper swung into view—a rickety, tiny wharf and a number of small brick and wooden buildings. The water became deeper, deep enough to accommodate fishing vessels, which was the reason that the village was situated there. A few dingy watercraft clustered along the shore, but Bolan's perusal didn't reveal the vessel he was searching for.

She was called *My Donna,* a high-powered, twenty-two-foot cruiser, with a fresh white paint job and new chrome railings that shone in the sun—at least, they had shone in the sun when Bolan had initially spotted the boat in the harbor at Cap Haitien. That was where he had last seen her, delivering her cargo to the Russians. Hal Brognola, director of Stony Man Farm, was able to give Bolan the name of her home port, and the soldier had always intended to follow her back to Barry Bay and to close down that link in the drug-trade chain. Now he was in search of information, such as what the Russians and the Cubans were up to.

The farther west he went, the less impressive Barry Bay looked, its outskirts scattered with shanty houses and battered rowboats tied to trees. The *My Donna* wasn't in sight. He dropped anchor and waited.

AN HOUR LATER *My Donna*'s wake slipped under the *Ocean Missed* and rocked her gently. The boat slowed abruptly and drifted toward a small, newer dock, where two men jumped out, one of them the short, dreadlocked black man who had piloted the ship into Cap Haitien. Bolan started his vessel and waited tensely as the men stood on the dock, conversing with another figure who arrived to greet them. There was a chance they would recognize the *Ocean Missed* if they gave her a good look, and would know instantly that something was very wrong. Bolan's best plan was to remain unnoticed by doing nothing.

From within the cover of the flying bridge he watched the three men converse. They disappeared into a stand of trees.

The sun was growing orange and approaching the horizon when Bolan disembarked. He was dressed in cutoff jeans, and in his waterproof pack he carried a dark T-shirt and shoes, along with his hardware, intending to pass himself off as an American tourist who had wandered from the resort.

He lowered himself into the water when the sun touched the flat line of the horizon, and swam effortlessly to shore, despite his backpack. He slowed as he approached the *My Donna,* but a few minutes of patience assured him no one remained on board. The craft was silent. The sun's last rays disappeared in a brilliant display that the soldier failed to notice as he crawled onto the weedy, rocky beach and, in the cover of the palms, dragged on his shirt. It clung to his wet skin, and the running shoes felt clammy as he pulled them on. He rubbed his hand on his shirt, drying it, and extracted the Beretta 93-R from the pack.

Bolan stepped onto a path leading from the dock through the trees, which cast long shadows as the sun sank in the west. He came to a single house on a large plot of mostly untended land. Through the trees he could make out the shanties of the poorest residents of Barry Bay. Somebody had cleared enough land to build this house recently, and with specific purpose. It was close to the town, but far enough away to offer some privacy. This was probably a section of the village where clandestine comings and goings could occur with little chance of notice by the local sheriff. The silence of these people would be easily purchased.

Bolan stepped through the sandy soil to one of the opened, screened windows. The flickering glow told him there was a TV on inside and no other lights. Crouching, he listened for conversation. There was a surge of canned laughter from a speaker and a snort from a live person. Bolan edged his head up into the window for a quick look.

A dreadlocked black man slumped on a battered easy chair before an old television blaring out an American sitcom. His head was propped on his fingers, and he seemed only very slightly entertained by the program.

Thinking he heard voices from another room, Bolan moved on, circling the house and finding a window that glowed with electric light. He crawled under it and listened again.

"This ain't too cool, man."

"Don't worry about it."

"I am worried about it. It's not cool. It's not right."

"We don't know what the problem is, do we? Let's just wait and see what they have to say when they call."

Bolan raised his head until he could see who was speaking. Two men occupied the room, both smoking. One was the short dreadlocked man from the boat, in his late forties judging by the lines on his face. The other was a younger black man with a shaved head.

"That's all we been doing, man, waitin' and waitin'. I'm tired of waitin'. I want the money that's owed me."

"You'll get it," the dreadlocked man said harshly.

"I don't think so. We should have told them we wanted to be paid when we delivered. I took a big chance delivering the coke with you, man."

"I know you did, and you'll be paid."

"Remind me again why we didn't get paid on delivery?"

"Yarling, I promise you these guys are in this thing for the long-term. They ain't going to screw us on one deal. They invested in this storage house and the boat, didn't they? They'd have nothing to gain by ripping us off now."

The shaven-headed man nodded as if he saw the logic in that, but he wasn't reassured and was about to speak again when the phone rang. Dreadlocks grabbed it.

"Yeah?" he asked, and listened. "So what was the screw-up... Tomorrow... Where... No, wait a second—I want to know—"

The conversation was over. Dreadlocks hung up.

"What's going on?" Yarling demanded.

"They want the hardware. They want us to deliver it to them at a meeting point just outside Jamaican waters tomorrow at noon."

Yarling was nodding, a grim look on his face. "Oh yeah, man? And I assume it's COD. We get paid for the coke and the guns when we get there, right?"

Dreadlocks didn't meet Yarling's eyes. "They didn't say."

"Did they explain to you what the sudden rush was? Did they tell you whether we're even getting paid at all?"

The other man was silent.

"This is bullshit, man! They're using us for their little go-get-'em boys! They ain't even paying us? Bullshit!"

"They'll pay us!"

"Why do you think that'll happen? Why should they pay us?"

"They need us! Think about it! They need people in place here to run this operation on a daily basis. They'll have to pay us because they know we won't work with them otherwise."

"Damn right. That includes delivering the guns tomorrow at noon. You go to the meeting if you want. You tell them they need to come up with the cash for the first little errand we do for them before they get the rest of their stuff."

"That's not a good idea, Yarling."

"What's the problem?" It was the TV-watcher, coming in to investigate the argument. Bolan chose that moment to leave his position and search for an entrance.

"We're getting ripped off, that's what!" Yarling shouted.

Dreadlocks was exasperated. "We are not getting ripped—"

"Fuck you!"

"Don't you talk to me like that—"

Yarling stomped to the couch where Dreadlocks perched and thrust a single finger into his chest. "I said fuck you!"

Bolan kicked the TV-watcher in the small of the back and sent him flying into the room with a grunt. He crashed to the floor at Yarling's feet. Yarling and Dreadlocks both looked at the man in the doorway in surprise, while the TV-watcher sprang to his feet with a cry, dragging an eight-inch fishing knife from the leather sheath in his belt and springing at Bolan. The Executioner slammed the fisted 93-R into the knife hand and swung the attacker into the doorjamb, which he hit with a heavy thud that sent him slumping to the ground. He bounced up again, swinging viciously at the soldier. The 93-R coughed once and the round traveled less than a yard before slamming the TV-watcher to the floor for a third and final time.

The Executioner was conscious of movement and knew he had ignored the two others for precious seconds. Yarling swore roundly as he grabbed for a sawed-off shotgun that leaned against a wall. The 93-R chugged out two rounds, and he collapsed heavily to the floor. He raised his head, spotted the shotgun and groped for it with nerveless fingers that knocked the weapon to the floor, where he stared at it as he died.

Dreadlocks reached for a small pistol he had tucked in his belt. He thought he had time enough to take out the white man while he dealt with the others, but the white man proved to be too fast. As he leveled his .38-caliber pistol, the large 9 mm handgun snapped into target acquisition on his chest and spoke once. The round drilled into his shoulder and seemed to explode, sending roaring, mangling tentacles of pain through his torso. He screamed and curled sideways on the couch, his .38 clattering on the plank floor.

Bolan yanked Dreadlocks into a sitting position, pushing the muzzle of the sound suppressor against his forehead where he could see it and feel it.

"Let me live! Let me live!"

"You're a drug smuggler. You don't deserve to live. But you're lucky. You're the last one alive who can explain to me what's going on around here."

Dreadlocks looked at him, hope in his pain-filled eyes.

"If you tell me the truth—and I mean the whole truth and nothing but the truth—then I might leave this place without firing this weapon again."

"I'm Jonny Smythe. Jonathon, they call me."

"I don't care what your name is. What are you doing here?"

"We're just cogs in the wheel, man! We got set up by some guys shipping cocaine and guns! We get it delivered to us from somebody, and we take it somewhere else!"

"And who set up this deal with you?"

"Some Russian guys. Major Rifkin was the main one. They gave us the money to have this house built and the dock." Smythe's body trembled and his eyes glazed over for a moment. "I'm hurt bad, man. You gotta help me!"

"Where's this Major Rifkin?"

"I don't know. I never knew anything about them. We were

shipping on our own, small-time loads of coke. They just showed up and made the deal with us. We only started doing the work for them last week, man! We only shipped one load of cocaine for them and we took in one load of guns. It's in the basement. It's why they made this house for us so we could install the basement—''

Another tremor shook his small form, and his eyes rolled into his skull.

''Take me to a doctor, man!'' he gasped.

''I'm not taking you anywhere.''

''You said you'd help me!''

''I said I wouldn't shoot you again.''

Bolan let the bleeding drug runner fall over again on the soggy couch as he began to search the house for the entrance to the basement. He was interrupted within minutes by the sound of the door, and he stepped into a dark corner until he saw a tall, muscular figure walk past him and head into the sitting area where the occupants lay. Bolan noticed that a Browning Hi-Power pistol was gripped in the newcomer's hand.

The Executioner stepped up behind the man, just out of arm's reach, and aimed squarely into the middle of the guy's back.

''Freeze or you're dead.''

The newcomer did, indeed, freeze, then chuckled deep in his throat. ''You aren't Russian. You're American.''

''Turn around slowly.''

The prisoner did as he was told, a smile touching his lips, letting the Hi-Power dangle gingerly from two fingers.

''You DEA, man?''

''No.'' Bolan snatched the pistol and moved back a pace. The man before him was a giant, towering over Bolan by several inches. He was Jamaican, with dreadlocks reaching the middle of his back. He was dressed in a lightweight, wheat-colored linen suit with a demure brown tie.

''CIA?''

''No. Who are you?''

"Jimmy Cie. Mo' Bay sheriff detective."

"Show me a badge. Slowly."

Cie reached for his identification with a steady, slow movement.

Bolan examined the badge and the photo ID, then waved Cie into the sitting room, where the detective immediately headed for the couch. The Executioner stepped over the shotgun corpse to get to a telephone, which he cradled against his shoulder and dialed. It took a full minute to get a connection outside of Jamaica, then another several seconds as various connections were made before ringing at the desk of Hal Brognola. It was late in Washington, but Bolan knew the big Fed would quite likely still be on the job. He worked long hours at the Justice Department and still had to keep abreast of what was going down at the Farm.

"Yeah?"

"Striker. I've got a Montego Bay, Jamaica, detective here named James Cie. I need to know if he's legit."

Bolan heard Brognola tap into his keyboard. The Justice Department databases were extensive. What wasn't directly accessible through Justice could be accessed through legitimate or illegitimate channels by the Stony Man computer staff. He kept an eye on the detective as he waited. But Cie seemed absorbed in tearing off Smythe's shirtsleeve and using it to apply pressure to the massive gunshot wound in the man's shoulder.

"Yeah. There's such a guy. Six-seven, thirty-three years old, dreadlocks."

Brognola recited details from a short bio on James Cie.

"Thanks."

"Know any more about this deal, Striker?"

"Not a thing. I'll check in later."

Cie stood as Bolan dropped the receiver.

"Who are you, American?"

"Belasko, Mike."

"Well, Mr. Belasko, if you're not CIA and you're not DEA, just who the hell are you?"

"I'm independent. If you need a number, I can give you one."

"Yeah? Well, you just independently killed three men in my country. Mind telling me what for?"

"I think you know what for," Bolan said. "You've had your eye on these guys yourself. Otherwise why would you be wandering around here in the dark?"

"You've got me there."

Bolan tossed the Hi-Power butt-first to Cie, who caught it and holstered it smoothly under his jacket, glancing at Bolan's Beretta. "That's a piece of work. But there were just the three of them. I think you don't need that anymore."

The Executioner ignored the suggestion. "I take it you've seen the Russians hanging around, too?"

"No, but the local kids have seen some Russians two or three times since they started building the house. I got the impression our boys were working with them. Seemed odd—but why shouldn't Russians be drug smugglers like anybody else?"

"Smythe told me this place was built recently, and that it has a basement for storage of smuggled goods. I was looking for the entrance when you showed up."

"Yeah. It's here. I know how to get in. You see, I've been after this bastard for about four years. He killed my first partner a long time ago and got off. So I watch everything he does. I watched them build this house—they didn't know it though. I know how to get into the basement."

He stepped back into the vestibule, inside the front door. "With the door closed, there's no way to see this part of the house from any window," Cie explained. He grabbed for a plank in the floor, his fingers dragging at it without affect. Then the plank slid sideways in its slot a quarter of an inch and he lifted it easily out of the floor.

A latch was revealed under the board. Cie opened it and swung up a large portion of the floor on three steel-hinged arms. The door into the floor leaned against the wall, a ramp stretching into the darkness below.

"I been watching them for months, now. But they just sat here for a long time doing nothing." Cie groped under the floor for a switch, and somewhere below an electric bulb lit up. "Then last week they got in their first shipment of cocaine. I was gonna bust them, but they moved the coke out too quick. So I waited. There's no way I was gonna chance closing in on them when they didn't have the goods. I wanted to put them away for a long time, see?"

"Sorry to take the pleasure away from you," Bolan said as he followed Cie down the ramp. Both of them were forced to duck under the ceiling.

The detective shrugged. "It is kind of anticlimactic, from my point of view. At least they've been stopped, one way or another. Good God!"

Cie stood in the middle of the dank concrete basement and stared at the boxes. Bolan was similarly impressed. The room was huge, far larger than he would have guessed, and stacked to the roof with dozens of wooden crates marked with Cyrillic characters.

Bolan finally did holster the 93-R and climbed halfway up one of the stacks. He grabbed the top box and pulled it off, sending it crashing to the rough concrete floor. It cracked and split open. Tufts of long wood shavings spilled out, along with the gleam of dark metal. Cie wrenched off the broken planks and withdrew a gleaming automatic weapon.

"What is this? I've never seen one of these before."

"AK-74 autorifle," Bolan said.

Cie held the piece as if he knew how but looked at Bolan. "Not an AK-47?"

"No. It fires a 5.45 mm round. The Soviets started using them in the early 1990s to replace the AK-47."

Cie frowned. "This looks newer than that, Belasko. In fact I'd guess this has never been fired."

Bolan nodded. "Factory-fresh. How many have we got?"

The detective quickly stooped and counted six weapons. Bolan was already making a count of the crates in the basement. They were stacked six high in four rows six deep.

Cie whistled long and low. "That's 864 automatic rifles."

Bolan said nothing, contemplating the implications.

The cop looked at the weapon in his hand as if he were suddenly afraid of it. "That's enough for any decent-sized army."

3

Colombia

General Ivan Resnikoff was irked at being kept waiting, but didn't show it. He played the game. One day there would come a time when no one would keep him waiting, including this Colombian lowlife, Quinones.

But right now he was in Colombia, in Quinones's house, where Quinones would be king.

The guard offered him coffee, then disappeared. Resnikoff knew he had been waiting a full fifteen minutes before the cartel head appeared.

"General! Good to see you again!"

Manny Quinones shook his hand briskly, with a big smile.

Resnikoff smiled thinly. "Yes, Mr. Quinones, it has been too long." Who did this third-world death-dealer think he was fooling, greeting him like he was an old friend? The truth was that they had met one time, years earlier, when Resnikoff had come to Cali. They hadn't spoken two words to each other.

But Resnikoff had remembered his name, and when Quinones became a figure of importance, the Russian was more than willing to leverage that brief, one-time meeting. If Quinones wanted to pretend they were old buddies, that was fine with him. He'd play along.

The Colombian was in a lightweight, open cotton shirt and slimming, pleated beige slacks, designed to hide his developing paunch. The man was letting the easy life get to him too quickly. That was the price of success for the weak-willed.

Quinones was unwilling to keep fighting for what was rightfully his and let others fight for him.

General Resnikoff wasn't that sort of a person. When he had achieved a level of status in the KGB, he had fought all that much harder to advance further.

When the USSR had illegally disbanded and tossed away decades of struggle in favor of the cheap, flashy lure of capitalism, Resnikoff had been among the brave few willing to fight for restoration of the old order, risking his very life in the coup attempt a few years earlier.

When the coup failed and Resnikoff was offered a position equal to his general's rank in the new order, he could have taken it and lived a life of ease as one of the elite of the new Russian government.

Such acquiescence wasn't a part of Resnikoff's nature.

Instead he had gone underground in Russia, taking up residence in places only he knew of, places he had established for himself years before, just in case he ever needed safe haven. It was a wise precaution as an upper-echelon member of one of the most dangerous organizations in the world.

Reaching out his tentacles in the underground, tentatively at first, Resnikoff had discovered he wasn't alone.

There were others from the former KGB in hiding, refusing to become a part of the new, illegal government of Russia. They were biding their time, waiting, watching, for their opportunity to make a change.

Resnikoff had waited with them, but he had his doubts. Russia was sustaining itself under its new form of government. There was a strong pro-Communist movement, but he was enough of a realist to see that it was ineffectual. True communism wouldn't be back. Not in Russia. Not anytime soon.

Resnikoff saw danger in waiting, too. His old comrades from the KGB and the Communist Party were getting lazy. Some rejoined society, taking places in the new government.

The general refused to go that route.

He was a Communist. He believed in Marxist-Leninist doctrines. He believed communism was the only true government of the people.

He found himself longing for the old days, when Mother Russia was the great and powerful Union of Soviet Socialist Republics and the KGB, behind the scenes, kept it running.

Resnikoff knew that living in the past was a dangerous obsession.

That was when he began to plan for his future.

For the future of communism.

He knew it was his responsibility to see that the purity of the Marxism-Leninism form of government was perpetuated.

Resnikoff's career included several long stints in the Republic of Cuba during the late 1970s and early 1980s, training members of the Dirección General de Inteligencia—the DGA—in KGB techniques. He had, of course, made a point of ferreting out those with points of view sympathetic to his own. He networked extensively and kept in touch through various channels with those he knew were like-minded.

He kept in touch with them even after the fall of the USSR. He knew that Cuba was in a dangerous position, that Castro was failing the people, that, inevitably, the people would turn against him and, desperate to improve their standard of living, they would embrace some new form of government. Under the onslaught of American propaganda, that new form of government would be capitalism.

Unless someone else came in first and showed them the error of the capitalist way.

It had come to Resnikoff one night as he lay in bed, tucked away in his tiny safehouse in Bihkova. He sat up in the darkness, suddenly awake, the logic and clarity of this course of action stunning him. He had laughed aloud in the darkness. He hadn't slept for two days after that, so great was his enthusiasm for the idea.

He and his people, loyal Communists, frustrated and displaced members of the KGB, would take control of the island nation of Cuba.

They would oust the old, ineffectual leader and his staff and put in place their own people. They would bring their expertise, learned during their years controlling the secret agencies of the Soviet Union, and use it to run the New Cuban Republic. They would make Cuba the new shining star of communism in a world where communism was dying a slow and agonizing death.

At once he had begun to contact his comrades from the former KGB. Within weeks he had located dozens of them, powerful men robbed of their rightful place, but retaining considerable knowledge and influence. Many of them were quick to see the promise of the future Resnikoff's plan held for the future and had joined him. Some wouldn't leave Russia but promised to support him however they could.

The former high-ranking officials of the KGB had their stashes of cash, and money from the secret Swiss bank accounts was offered.

More important was the hardware that became available. Resnikoff had his own store of weapons and secret matériel, and so, it appeared, did many of the ex-KGB majors and generals who offered him assistance. So did the ex-army and ex-navy personnel who came to his aid. Some of them, in fact, were still in the Russian army and navy, yet were willing to make hardware available to Resnikoff.

The biggest problem became the logistics of assembling it all.

Then Resnikoff located Reunion Island.

The small island was a private estate, but the British banker who owned it had suffered some financial hardships in years past. He neglected to insure the island and had suffered the further misfortune of an almost direct hurricane hit during the summer of 1995. The house and grounds had been wrecked, and had lain in their destroyed state for a year when Resnikoff discovered it. He offered a paltry sum for the dot of Caribbean land, and the British banker was glad to get it.

The estate house remained where it had fallen. Or so it seemed. Under the wreckage Resnikoff began to build barracks and storehouses. He began to amass his hardware there, and brought in his most loyal ex-KGB friends to help him make his dream a reality.

He began to plan for the taking of Cuba.

First he needed an army that would do his work.

"So you need some men?" Manuel Quinones said. He poured vodka into glasses on the table, then handed one to his guest.

Resnikoff nodded and drank deeply. A mark of Russian pride was the ability to drink Russian vodka with gusto. This stuff was so smooth and so filtered—perfect for soft American tastes—that it was like drinking water. "Yes. You know my plans. You know what I intend to do."

Quinones nodded. "Well, you've told me some of what you plan and I can guess the rest, General. I need to know a little more."

"What more can I tell you?"

"About your friends in Cuba, mostly. I understand you spent some time there and you have contacts. I think you will need more than contacts in Cuba in order to accomplish your goals."

Resnikoff nodded and sat back in his chair, crossing his legs and putting a hand on his ankle, a formal pose that he knew would impress these casual, underdressed South Americans. "You are correct, Mr. Quinones. My leverage in Cuba is the key to my success. As you've guessed, I have more than 'contacts' in Cuba. I have some very close professional relationships there. I know some of the most important players in the Cuban government, people whose names are virtually unknown outside of the island. Nevertheless, they are the real power players.

"I have been in regular contact with them since my days in Cuba over a decade ago. I carefully selected those who I knew would be enthusiastic about my plan. They have created their own links of sympathizers. Our network has become extensive."

"You say this is the key to your success? Explain this to me."

"We'll start with the double execution of the president and vice president—that act is my responsibility solely. Once we've taken that step, our inside people will institute a series of simultaneous surgical strikes, effectively amputating the vital limbs of the old government and installing our own all at one time. The members of the new government heads, for example, have been chosen. The old government will cease to exist and the new government will take its place within the course of a few hours. During a very short time frame the upper ranks of the Revolutionary Navy, the Air Defense Force, the Territorial Militia Troops, the Youth Labor Army, the Interior Ministry Border Guard Troops, and even the DGA will be replaced by men loyal to our cause. The success of our strike in Havana will trigger strikes in Santiago de Cuba, Camaguey, Santa Clara, Pinar del Rio, Holguin, Guantánamo, Matanzas, and Cienfuegos. As you can see, this will need to be a highly coordinated series of events."

"It sounds extremely complicated. And it seems that every step of your process depends on the success of the former step. Especially at the outset. How will you be able to get at the president and vice president, I wonder?" Quinones asked. "In fact I wonder how well you'll be able to bring it all together under a single command."

Resnikoff smiled. "A fair question. But remember, we're working with the top men from the largest secret government agency that has ever existed. We're accustomed to organizing extensive, multinational covert operations that run efficiently and effectively. Let me add that we have access to some of the most advanced communication and military equipment the Soviet Union ever produced during its last great decade, literally some of the most advanced equipment of its kind ever made."

"Purchased with money you made selling my cocaine?" Quinones asked with a laugh.

Resnikoff smirked. He was still blistering from the loss of the cocaine, not to mention the loss of the Cuban general, Narciso Solas, and his own Russian friend, Major Alex Sablin.

He still hadn't received a satisfactory explanation as to what happened. But he wasn't about to let this third-worlder know the truth.

"Yes, as a matter of fact, we will be using those dollars to arm our compatriots in Cuba. The narcotics will be sold on the streets of Havana and other cities and used to purchase soldiers for the early strikes. We will not need those soldiers after we've started the ball rolling. You see, I fully expect the people of Cuba will join in our revolution the moment they know of it.

"We will change Cuba, make it a Marxist-Leninist nation, removing it from the shackles of a monocultural economy that has starved its people of prosperity for decades. We will develop copper, nickel, iron ore and timber resources, and we'll provide opportunities for the educated. Cuba will change from a dying nation into the model of success that will motivate a series of new Communist revolutions. The twenty-first century will be the Century of Hope that the twentieth might have been, had not the dictators and the zealots betrayed the Marxist vision."

Quinones laughed and slapped the table. "You're a man with a mission, General. You've thought of everything, as far as I can tell."

Resnikoff smiled. "I have."

"I am so impressed with this plan of yours, in fact, that I have a deal to offer you. A deal that is contingent on your success. It will mean long-term benefits for both of us."

Resnikoff stiffened and listened.

Quinones noted the sign of interest and proceeded. "I think you're going to do it. I really do. At least, I am confident enough to seriously consider giving you the men you want, even though it will mean a substantial slowdown in my own operation.

"What I would like to suggest is this—instead of leasing my men as you have suggested, I would like to make a barter. You get all my top men. After you have achieved your goal,

I get free use of a port in Cuba from which to conduct my business for a period of ten years.''

Resnikoff bristled. "You want to use Havana as a staging ground for importing cocaine into the United States?"

"Right. I would need absolutely free access, of course. No restrictions.''

"You must be joking!"

"General, why would you think I am joking?" Quinones asked evenly.

"I can't allow my new home nation to be a port for illegal drug trade!''

"Excuse me, General, but didn't you just send something like three hundred kilos of cocaine into your new home nation?"

"That was for the war effort. Such compromises have to be made sometimes. But once we're in control, we'll assemble a nation based on the doctrines of Marxist-Leninist theory, and they allow no room for drug smuggling.''

"I am not asking for permission to sell within Cuba, General. I'll simply use Cuba as a staging ground. Look at it as a method for creating further ruin to your great enemy, the United States.''

Resnikoff pushed back in his chair suddenly. "I am sorry, Mr. Quinones, but it is out of the question. I had no idea this is what you had in mind. I am sorry for wasting your time.''

"Wait, wait! It was an idea, General, not an ultimatum.''

Resnikoff said nothing. Suddenly he saw the Colombian for what he really was—a slimy capitalist profiting on human misery. Resnikoff felt filthy for having to interact, let alone bargain with him.

"Let's see what kind of a purely financial arrangement can be made,'' Quinones offered.

Resnikoff sat for a moment, then nodded. "Yes. Let's.''

ANTONY MAYER WOKE when the sun shone through his window and walked out the back door to the bushes, scratching his stomach and yawning. The morning was cool enough that it chilled him, and he rubbed his arms as he finished his business and turned back to the shack he called home.

And realized there were no less than four men standing there watching him.

One of them was Joseph J. The rest were his boys. That meant trouble.

"Joseph J., how ya doing, man?" Mayer said as jovially as possible while assessing the possibilities of successful flight.

"Not too good, Antony. We come to see you because of what you been doing and we aren't too happy about it."

"What are you talking about? I haven't been stepping on your boys' toes," Mayer protested. One of the boys with Joseph J. was a lanky local fellow named Steven, a track star at one time. No way was Mayer going to get away by running. There was no way he was going to get away at all.

"You know that's not true, Antony," Joseph J. said, sucking on a joint so that his cheeks caved into his face and gave it the appearance of a bare skull. "You've been recruiting boys in our town for dirty work."

"Yeah, so what? I been giving boys jobs, that's all. Boys that haven't got jobs. Those boys are sending money home to their folks now, where they weren't making no money before."

"But you've been doing it in our town, Antony."

Mayer crossed his arms across his shirtless chest and tucked his hand in his armpits. Joseph J. and his boys were moving in slowly, almost casually. "I've been doing it in *my* town. And I haven't been cutting into your business in any way."

"Everything in this town is my business, and that's what you fail to understand."

"How's my business hurting your business?" Mayer demanded desperately as Joseph J. stopped directly in front of him.

"Let me explain it to you, Antony."

Joseph J.'s fist appeared out of nowhere and slammed into Mayer's stomach, moving so fast he didn't have time to sidestep it. He doubled over with a grunt of pain, staggering for a moment. He opened his eyes and saw the ground, and then there was a foot moving rapidly into his field of vision. Pain exploded in his face. He felt more than heard a crunch of breaking bone and saw a spray of red drops in the air as he collapsed onto his back.

After that he lost track of the hits. All he knew was that one burst of pain after another rocked his body for what seemed like hours.

Then there was a scream from far away. It was a woman, hysterical. She was shouting about dead bodies. It attracted the attention of Joseph J. and his boys, who went to investigate the commotion. Mayer rolled onto his knees and vomited, then stood on shaky legs and staggered into the brush.

THE LEASED JET had been chosen for its conservative, corporate look and its high speed capacity. The twin-engine jet made the flight from Neiva, Colombia, to Belize in the time it took for Resnikoff to enjoy a leisurely in-flight meal. It set down in the city of Orange Walk in late afternoon.

His driver, like his pilot, was ex-KGB, men Resnikoff had employed since before the fall of the USSR. They were men he trusted. The driver fetched their rented Jeep Grand Cherokee, and they drove into the countryside.

One of the distinct advantages of the operation in the Caribbean was its proximity to a seemingly endless supply of soldiers-for-hire. The troubles in Central and South America and the lucrative drug trade had created an abundance of fighting groups, few of them married to specific ideals. They'd fight for whatever cause paid well enough. A sign of moral decrepitude, Resnikoff knew, but not something that bothered him so much he wouldn't avail himself of their skills.

In fact he saw a number of advantages in fighting with mercenaries hired from the region. They were expendable, they brought their own hardware and they didn't need to be promised a stake in the new Cuba once the fighting was over.

That was the worst aspect of the logistics of his undertaking—appeasing all the parties involved. Every Russian and every Cuban wanted a slice of the pie. He had already promised more than he had to offer to his Cuban allies in terms of military control. He had no intention of allowing Cuba to be in control of any armed forces after he was in charge.

The New Cuban Republic was going to be more Russian than any of his Cuban allies realized.

But this night he'd have to negotiate nothing more than salary.

The road became rougher the farther they drove from the city. The merc band he was going to visit made its home much of the time on the Mexican border of Belize. It meant easy access to the national border and a short drive to Guatemala. Even Honduras and El Salvador were just hours away. This band would be tough to track for most authorities.

Resnikoff was scheduled to meet two Americans who led the group: Gary Albrecht, group leader, and Brian Fagen. They were buddies from childhood who had joined the Marines together, received multiple citations and got kicked out together. The details of their dishonorable discharges were unclear; what was no secret was that the two men no longer spent time in the U.S.

The general didn't care what their politics were. He knew they were for hire, and so was their band of trained soldiers. Money would buy their loyalty, although funds were starting to run dry.

Nobody knew how short on cash Resnikoff really was, which was the real reason he had needed the drug money from the Cubans so badly. The loss of the drugs infuriated him, more than the deaths of Sablin and Solas.

He wanted an explanation. He assumed someone had attacked them. But two heavily armed boats—what could attack them and live through it? DEA, perhaps?

He might never know. But if he ever found out who had cost him all that money, he would shoot him through the heart, no questions asked, and rejoice over his dead body.

He was KGB. Heart and soul. Nobody challenged a KGB general and lived to brag about it.

4

Bolan disliked waiting. He was a man of action. On the other hand, he'd slept little in the past thirty-six hours and was determined to make good use of the time to rest and gain strength.

He didn't like having to leave the automatic weapons where they were, but he didn't have the means to destroy them. The detective, Jimmy Cie, had promised the Jamaican police would take custody of the weapons, and Bolan had almost gone along with the idea.

Then he changed his mind. The close to nine hundred automatic weapons weren't going to be removed from the house without quite a bit of local attention, especially after the discovery of the bodies. Whoever in town knew about those weapons—and surely there was someone—would notify the owners not to bother to come looking for them if the Jamaican government took them away.

But if the bodies were removed without the weapons, somebody would eventually sneak into the house to get them, and that somebody might very well know who had arranged for the weapons to be in that basement.

It was information Bolan was extremely interested in, which meant he had to sit and wait.

ANTONY MAYER MIXED with the crowd and watched the removal of the bodies. A constable from Montego Bay came along with a sheriff's detective and searched the place, roped it off and dusted for fingerprints. Eventually they left the scene.

The villagers milled about for a while, but there was really nothing else to see, so they left the house of death.

In the late afternoon Mayer returned. He crept to the far side of the trees before entering from a point that was out of sight of the village and advanced slowly, carefully searching for others. Seeing no one, he at last ducked under the yellow police tape and entered the house.

He waited inside the door for a long minute. When there was no cry of alarm, he began to explore.

There was blood in several places, but not as much as he would have expected from three dead men. Some furniture was out of place, traces of fingerprint powder lay everywhere. But the planks where the floor opened looked undisturbed.

So the guns were still there—unless whoever killed the three men took the weapons and replaced the flooring carefully.

Mayer had to know. He had to report everything to Major Rifkin.

He removed the plank, grabbed the trapdoor, listened for a moment longer, then opened it carefully and started down the steps into the darkness. He reached up for the light switch as he passed.

AFTER A GOOD NIGHT'S sleep aboard the *Ocean Missed,* Bolan came to shore and regained his perch as the last of the curious onlookers dissipated. At the top of the palm tree he kicked out a family of rats and settled into a comfortable position to wait. He didn't wait long.

The tall, lanky villager stepped from tree to tree with obvious caution. He never thought to look up into the trees and entered the house assuming he was alone.

Bolan slid down the tree and entered the house with quick, silent steps, just in time to see the trapdoor open and the light go on below. That told him the villager was in the know. He doubted this was the man behind the operation—he was probably just a local hireling.

But he might know how to contact the guy in charge.

The light in the basement went out. Bolan retreated and hid behind the building. When the man left the house again, as carefully as he had come, he never dreamed he had a tail.

ANTONY MAYER SPOTTED Joseph J. leaning against a porch post outside the bar across the street, sipping from a bottle of beer. He gave Mayer a glare but didn't seem inclined to continue the beating he'd started earlier.

Mayer headed to the market, where there was a pay phone on a pole, and dialed a number that linked him to a hotel room in Montego Bay.

"Where've you been Mayer?" Major Vasily Rifkin demanded. "I've been expecting you to report in for hours."

"You heard the bad news, boss? I been trying to find out more than the police know about the killings."

"Well? What did you find out?" Rifkin snapped.

"I just snuck inside the house. All the police have left now. I went below to see about the guns. They're still there."

"Still there?" Rifkin repeated. "That doesn't make sense. I assumed those men had been killed *for* the guns."

"So did I, boss, but they're still there. Every single crate, as far as I can tell. Not one missing."

"Then who killed those men?" Rifkin asked.

"That I can't tell you."

There was silence on the line for a long ten seconds.

"I want you to try to find out, Mayer. Talk to people. See if anybody has a clue who killed those men. If you find out anything at all, contact me."

"Well, I've had some problems of my own, boss...." Mayer said hesitantly.

"What do you mean?"

Mayer explained his rough treatment at the hands of Joseph J. and his boys. "They want me to stop recruiting for you, boss. If I start nosing around, I'll get beat again for sure."

Another protracted silence. "No, you won't, Antony. I have men on the way to Barry Bay. They'll off-load the guns after dark. Before they do, you point out your friend Joseph J. They'll take care of things. I don't want you reducing your recruitment pace.''

''You want me to keep working out of this town, boss?''

''Of course.''

Mayer hung up, wearing a broad grin at the thought of the major sending his soldiers to deal with Joseph J. This would be sweet revenge. Mayer knew Rifkin's men were some of the scariest, toughest sons of bitches on the island.

Joseph J. wouldn't stand a chance.

Speaking of tough-looking SOBs, there was a white man standing nearby looking at a tourist map. The guy was dark, tall, with eyes that glinted like gunmetal. Not your typical tourist. He didn't give Mayer more than a glance as he stepped to the phone.

AFTER DUSK Joseph J. was still out front of the bar, drinking his beer and feeling lazy. Not much was going on that evening.

The truth was, he was feeling a little insecure. The day had started out well enough, flexing a little muscle on Antony Mayer, but the killings had disturbed him. Gunplay like that was out of Joseph J.'s league. Whoever had committed the murders was vicious, arrogant—somebody so powerful that he didn't care that he was operating in claimed territory.

Either way, it made Joseph J. feel like a low man on the ladder. He didn't like that at all. He preferred being in a position of power. The citizens in this town respected him because he was young, aggressive, ruthless.

Maybe he needed to do some more flexing and make a better reputation for himself, really beat the shit out of a few people and spread the word that Joseph J. was definitely not the man to mess with.

That was a good idea, and Antony Mayer was the ideal target for setting an example. He'd take care of it the following day.

''Later on,'' he said with a wave of his empty bottle. The

three men squatting on the ground playing poker mumbled in reply.

Joseph J. started to walk.

He took only two steps before he stopped again.

There were five men coming toward him through the empty village square, emerging from the darkness with the biggest guns Joseph J. had ever seen. All the guns were aimed directly at him.

"What's going on?" Joseph J. demanded.

"Shut up or I'll shoot you dead right now." The lead man came within two paces of Joseph J. as the others urged his surprised companions to their feet. Their cries of outrage were silenced by quiet threats.

The four young men stood in a line. The five gunmen faced them, all Caucasian, all in vaguely military looking outfits unadorned by rank or identifying insignia.

"We hear that you have been bothering a friend of ours," the lead man stated. To Joseph J. the accent sounded Eastern European, like Czech or Russian, although he had never met anyone from either of those countries.

"We don't know any friends of yours, man," Joseph J. protested.

"Really? You laid hands on him this morning."

"Mayer?" Joseph J. was so stunned he forgot for a moment to be scared. How could that little shit Mayer be tied to evil bastards like this?

"Mayer," the leader agreed. "You will never bother him again."

"We won't, man, we won't," said one of Joseph J.'s boys, almost sobbing. "We didn't know, that's all. We won't touch him again! Never!"

"You are right. You never will."

All five of the AK-74 automatic rifles fired simultaneously.

BOLAN STOOD in the shadows and observed.

He knew who the four locals were. He knew they were drug

dealers, hoods, maybe even killers. Maybe the Russians were intending to kill them, but Bolan didn't get involved.

He wasn't about to risk everything to save a handful of dealers. There was something much bigger at stake.

What it was, precisely, he couldn't say yet.

Cuban generals. Russians. Enough Soviet hardware to equip an army. Drug deals and secret stashes in a poor Jamaican village. Puzzle pieces were grouped together on the table, but formed no coherent picture.

Bolan needed more pieces. He knew just where to get them.

The four villagers lay on the ground moaning, crying and rolling into one another. To a man their knees had been so shot up they would never walk again. There would be no saving their legs.

The Russians stalked through the village and back into the darkness, ignoring the cries of alarm and the lights coming on. They were confident there was no one around who would risk messing with them.

Bolan followed them at about twenty paces as they headed into the copse of trees to a small motorized launch. The villager who had snuck into the house earlier in the day was waiting for them there nervously.

"Did you get them?"

"We got them, Mr. Mayer," the lead Russian said. "You will have no further interference from those four men."

"You didn't kill them, did you?" Mayer asked nervously.

"No, but they'll never walk again."

"So, what now?"

"Now, Mr. Mayer, you help us load those guns. In the morning you go back to recruiting men for us. Just like before."

"I got you twelve men already. How many more you gonna want me to get you?"

"More than you can possibly get for us. Don't feel as if you're going to reach a limit, because it is not going to happen. We are doubling your finder's fee to three hundred dollars a head."

Mayer stood in the moonlight and drew a broad grin. "That's fine with me."

"And we're upping the pay for all recruits to five hundred dollars per month. That should increase your business."

"Yeah, it sure will."

"Let's start loading the guns."

Bolan moved deeper among the palm trees with the skill of an experienced jungle warrior. The sandy soil and the sparse underbrush made silent approach easier. Still, he carried the Beretta 93-R drawn and ready to fire.

He would have to work this operation carefully. He needed information, and he couldn't afford to allow five Russians, plus the local man, to gun for him all at once. Those were tough odds for anyone, no matter how skilled. He watched from the shadows as the first crates were dollied to the dock and loaded onto the launch. The vessel was a small motorboat, which left the dock and headed for a larger craft anchored about a mile out to sea, beyond the coral reef that encircled the island.

Two men were in the launch. The other four worked in teams of two, each with a dolly, bringing crates to the dock. They were in for a long night of hard work.

If they lived through it.

The first team appeared with a dolly loaded with crates—it was one of the Russian gunmen and the Russian leader. Bolan stepped into the open, a moving, dark shadow in the moonlight, which gleamed off the tranquil ocean. The Russians didn't hear him and didn't see him until he was within ten paces and made his presence known.

"Stop. Hands in the air."

The hardman looked up, startled, but the leader flew into motion, stepping behind the upright dolly and grabbing at a shoulder holster. Bolan deked to the left, defeating the Russian's attempt to shield himself, and triggered the 93-R, which spit out three rounds. One of the 9 mm parabellum rounds slammed into the wooden crate with a crunch, while two drilled into the Russian, who whirled in the sand like a dervish and landed on all fours, his hands clutching convulsively at the sand. As the man continued to scrabble for his weapon, the Executioner fired again, all three rounds hitting their target squarely in the back. The leader was crushed to the ground.

Bolan spun to the other gunman, who had made a grab for the AK he had slung on his back and had nearly achieved target acquisition before Bolan proved his speed. The burst of rounds from the 93-R tore into the gunman's chest, knocking him off his feet and cracking his shoulders into the ground, the AK-74 falling next to him.

The Executioner stood still and listened. He judged he had less than a minute before the next team appeared: another Russian gunman and the Jamaican, Mayer. He holstered the 93-R with a single movement and grabbed at the Russian leader, dragging him quickly into the trees. The dead gunman went next, then Bolan ran into the open, scraping away the drag trails with his feet. There was little he could do about the black marks in the sand where puddles of blood had soaked. As he grabbed at the fallen AK he heard voices behind him on the path. He retreated into the trees, standing over his victims.

The Russian and the Jamaican appeared with their dolly of gun crates and stopped next to the abandoned dolly.

"Where have they gone?" the Russian asked, not immediately alarmed.

"To take a whiz?"

The Russian gave Mayer a glare that told him he doubted his two comrades would have gone into the woods together to make water.

"Major?" he said loudly. He turned and looked in the other direction, away from Bolan, who took a step in the open as he configured the 93-R to single-shot fire and aimed carefully. There was a burst and a single round chopped into the ankle of the Jamaican, who shouted in pain and fled into the trees. As the Russian spun, his AK ready to fire, Bolan shot into the biceps of his trigger arm—halting any potential unsuppressed gunfire was his immediate intention. The gun flopped forward in the Russian's hand as he shouted. Bolan fired again and the Russian dropped to the ground.

He sprang into the trees, but he could hear the crashing flight of the Jamaican far ahead—he'd failed to slow the man with his leg shot. But it didn't matter. Mayer wouldn't be back, and he wasn't important in the scheme of things.

He grabbed the fallen Russian and dragged him into the shadows of the trees to join his dead companions.

The sound of the launch traveled over the water within minutes, and Bolan spotted it heading toward the dock. The two Russians aboard saw nothing on shore to alarm them. They docked the launch and the pilot killed the engine while his companion jumped out and looped the mooring ropes onto the dock posts. He dragged the heavy ramp into position while the pilot stepped onto the dock and headed for the crates.

Bolan aimed carefully from the darkness and fired one time. The ramp-mover shouted and tumbled off the dock, landing face first in the water.

The boat pilot laughed derisively and spoke in Russian as he walked back to his companion. He paused and spoke again. The man was floating facedown in the shallow water, and a dark stain was spreading around him. The lone surviving Russian gave a shout of alarm.

"Don't move," Bolan said, stepping onto the dock. The Russian ignored his order and spun, trying to bring his AK-74 into firing position. But the 93-R was already aimed, and the Executioner triggered it once, sending a single round into the Russian's gut. He walked three steps backward, his face a mask of shock in the pale moonlight, and fell on his back.

With the big handgun aimed squarely at the Russian's heart, Bolan leaned over and relieved the man of his automatic weapon, tossing it unceremoniously into the sea where it sank instantly. The Russian grunted and observed his attacker with agonized hatred.

"All right, I've wasted enough time here," Bolan said quietly. "I want to know who you are and what the deal is."

The Russian groaned, but a tiny smirk appeared at the corner of his mouth. "Fuck you, American."

"Wrong answer." The 93-R moved slightly in his hand and fired one time, ripping a chunk of flesh from the outside of the Russian's thigh.

The Russian bit off the scream of pain that threatened to burst from his throat. He grabbed at the fresh wound, then stared at his shining wet hand.

Bolan leaned over the bloodied Russian so that he could see the handgun through his pain. "I'm not offering you another chance."

"I'll tell you!" the Russian gritted.

"Good. Who are you? Who's your leader?"

"I am ex-Soviet army. Our leader's KGB."

"There is no more KGB," Bolan said flatly.

"Ex-KGB! We are Communists. We believe in the Soviet Union! Not in the capitalist Russia of today!"

"So what are you doing here? Why are you selling drugs and arms?"

"We are not selling the guns! We're selling drugs to fund our New Revolution. We need the guns to equip our army."

"A new Russian revolution? I don't buy it."

The gunman gasped in pain. He was bleeding excessively from his wounds, and Bolan knew he wouldn't last long.

"Not Russia, Cuba. We are going to take over Cuba. Make it a new Marxist power. Remove the leaders there now—they have betrayed the Marxist philosophy. We will build a new Communist superpower!"

Bolan considered this carefully. "How many men are involved?"

"Many men. I don't know. Many ex-KGB. Many ex-Soviet military. You could never find us all. We have Soviet equipment. We have Cuban allies. You won't stop us—and when we succeed, and the Cuban people have united under us—then you Americans will have cut your own throats. You thought you eradicated the USSR as your hostile enemy, but we will be back at close proximity with all the weapons your President tried to keep out of Cuba thirty-five years ago!'' The Russian was ranting, losing his grip on reality, shuddering with cold in the warm tropical evening as his wounds drained his life strength.

"Where is your leader? Where's your base of operations?"

The Russian croaked, deep in his throat, "Fuck you, American!" He no longer saw Bolan or the threat of the 93-R.

His eyes closed.

Bolan dragged him and his floating companion into the trees with the others. All the while he was thinking hard.

A new Communist superpower in Cuba.

It made some kind of sense. The leadership in Cuba was no longer regarded as effective, not even by the Communist Party. There had to be a strong contingent in the Party, and in all the branches of the military, that would welcome new leadership, especially experienced, orthodox Marxist-Leninist leaders.

Bolan had seen evidence firsthand of high-level Cubans co-operating with the plan.

He also knew firsthand about the KGB, knew how strong an organization it had been and how entrenched the various factions of the KGB were. He had no doubts that there were KGB leaders who had socked away millions of dollars. Who knew how much hardware they had secreted into clandestine strongholds, especially during the last few years of the Soviet Union, when it became clear that communism's days, and the days of the KGB, were numbered?

Even after the disintegration of the organization, the men involved, with all their power and influence, had continued to operate under new organizational structures—or outside them. They would be able to access hardware belonging to what was essentially the second-greatest military body on the planet. If they were still Communists at heart, they could easily feign loyalty to the new Russia while channeling hardware and cash into whatever cause they believed in. After the failure of the hard-liners' coup attempt, many of them would have come to believe there was no future for a Communist Russia. So they would look for another home.

Bolan knew that with enough firepower, Cuban allies, disenfranchised soldiers from the Caribbean, and ready cash, nothing could stop a takeover of Cuba.

Unless Bolan could halt the attempt before it started.

He needed to alert Jimmy Cie. Now it was more imperative than ever that these guns get locked up where they couldn't be used.

He needed to contact Brognola, find out what he could tell him about these KGB agents: who they were, what they actually had in the way of backing and Cuban alliances.

He had to find that base of operations, which was his next priority.

There was somebody nearby who could provide that information.

ANTONY MAYER TAPED UP the wounded ankle and drank from a bottle of rum, but it seemed the pain would never go away. He huddled on his bed in the corner under a blanket, chilled to the bone, waiting for sunrise.

Then there was movement in the darkness and he screamed.

"Quiet, Mr. Mayer."

"Who are you, man?"

"I'm the guy who did that." The shadowy figure gestured with the huge handgun at Mayer's distended, throbbing foot.

"What do you want from me?"

"The Russians are all dead."

Mayer digested that unpleasant information. "What do you want from me?"

"I want to know where you were sending the men you're recruiting for the Russians."

"On a boat. Out of Jamaica."

"Where?"

"I don't know where."

The hand holding the big handgun stopped moving casually

and seemed to become rigid. "Mr. Mayer, the Russians are dead. Why do you think I'll hesitate to kill you?"

"Reunion Island! We ship the boys out of here once a week!"

"Good. You won't be recruiting any more men for the Russians, Mr. Mayer."

The man nodded and squinted, trying to see the face of the intruder, but he was only a mass of darkness in the unlit hut. "I won't."

"There will be a Jamaican detective coming to visit you tomorrow. His name is Jimmy Cie. You will cooperate with him in every way. If you give him any trouble, or if you hold anything back, he'll tell me. Understand?"

"I got it, I got it! Who the hell are you, anyway, man?"

The dark figure stepped backward into the shadows and disappeared.

5

Angolan Coast, Africa

The aircraft carrier *Admiral Kuznetsov* rumbled northward, just out of sight of the city of Lobito. Captain Yakov Frudkin enjoyed the smooth, dry feel of the warm air. He dragged on his French cigarette and watched the horizon, bare and empty, but always holding promise.

He expected no activity today, just exercises and simulations. In fact he didn't expect real action in the foreseeable future. The world was awfully peaceful these days from a Russian point of view. Not that he was a warlike man, but he'd welcome a little excitement to stir things up, to keep his men on edge and prevent the inexorable softness of peacetime.

"Captain Frudkin?" The yeoman with the headphones leaned back in his chair. "Message for you, sir. For your ears only."

Interesting. But probably nothing. Mundane messages became high-priority and top-secret when there was nothing really important going on. He took the headset.

"Frudkin."

"This is a message from Admiral Erik Karamalikov, priority 'Alpha,' authorization zed."

Frudkin said nothing, but his heart beat a little faster. There was a breath at the other end of the line. "You are to send two Yak Forger VTOLs to the following coordinates immediately. This is not a drill, Captain. Pilots will be directed to await instructions upon arrival at those coordinates."

"Armed?"

"Of course, Captain—as I said, this is not a drill."

Frudkin contemplated the instructions. An admiral's orders with special authorization were beyond questioning. The co-ordinates would put his jets somewhere deep in southern Angola. From there they might be sent anywhere. There were any number of African powder-keg situations that might have flared up and caught the attention of Moscow.

"Yes, sir," Frudkin said. "Anything else, sir?"

"No, Captain. I suggest you make haste."

YURIY TROSCHENKOVA had been going quietly insane for days waiting for the summons. Every time he heard a call over the loudspeakers he thought it would be *his* call.

Suddenly, like a bolt of lightning, *his* call came.

Vasja Kolokatov arrived a moment later, opening his locker and scrambling for his flight suit.

"What do you suppose is happening?"

Troschenkova shook his head, almost casually. "Another exercise," he suggested, hoping his comrade didn't see his shaking hands or the glint of heart-pounding excitement in his eyes.

"It doesn't sound like an exercise."

Troschenkova shrugged, feeling a pang of guilt. Kolokatov would die this day, which was too bad. They'd been friends for years, since they met during training on the Forgers. He was an excellent pilot, as well. It would have been good to have him on their side.

Troschenkova had done his best. He had started by dropping hints, stating his opinion about the fall of communism and the failure of the new governments that had been put in place. Finally he had come out and told his friend that he felt like a traitor serving what he considered to be an illegal government.

Kolokatov hadn't agreed. He had his doubts about the success of the capitalist economy—he had cousins and friends who were living well below their old standards—but things had gotten better than they had in the early days after communism's disintegration in Russia, he pointed out. The shops had food again. There were signs of steady improvement.

Troschenkova had suggested that there might be a new USSR for them to serve, but his friend had only laughed and said he wouldn't serve it.

Troschenkova had been very sad when he heard those words, which had signed his friend's death warrant.

Kolokatov gave his comrade a grin as they crossed the tarmac to the waiting VTOLs. "Fly straight, my friend!"

The other man nodded, and tried to smile in return. "Fly well." It was a traditional exchange they had developed during their early days of training together.

The two pilots waited as the ground crew operators brought the Forgers roaring to life and climbed out. Troschenkova sat in his bird and began to feel a resurgence of his excitement.

He was sorry about his friend, but it was a price that had to be paid. He'd feel bad about it, but his mourning would be outweighed by the elation of being a part of the New Revolution.

They received clearance from control, and he fed fuel to the engines of the Forgers. The lifter thrust hit the flight deck, and both craft levitated smoothly, monstrously loud and huge, like twin steel dragons. Troschenkova fed more fuel to the Koliesov lift engines, and he began to move slowly away from the *Admiral Kuznetsov,* out over the Atlantic Ocean. The cruise engines created greater thrust and the jets accelerated, rocketing east over the water, quickly leaving the massive carrier behind them. Soon they were reaching six hundred miles per hour and approaching an altitude of ten thousand feet.

Troschenkova's headphones crackled and got his attention. "New orders," said the radioman on the *Admiral Kuznetsov.* "No change of destination. But complete radio silence is mandated until you are contacted upon arrival. Understood?"

The two pilots signed off.

They were on their own.

The Forgers leveled off at thirty-six thousand feet.

THE RADIO CRACKLED to life again as they crossed 16° south latitude. The order was brief and to the point—land and await contact.

Their destination was a patch of dry wasteland in the middle of nowhere. A camouflaged truck sat on a dirt road. Four soldiers killed time watching the Forgers as they came to a hovering halt, hanging forty feet in the air briefly before descending gently to the cracked soil.

Troschenkova cut the engines, wondering if his friend was totally dismayed at these events.

He climbed to the ground and the soldiers approached, Kalashnikovs slung over their shoulders.

A Russian army major wearing black sunglasses exited the truck. He approached the two pilots as they removed their flight helmets and saluted smartly.

"Lieutenant Troschenkova, Lieutenant Kolokatov." He didn't introduce himself.

The pilots returned the salute.

"Lieutenant Troschenkova, any luck?" the major asked.

"No, Major."

"I'm sorry to hear that."

"Me, too, sir."

The major reached for the handgun on his belt, drew it quickly and leveled it at Vasja Kolokatov's chest without hesitation.

Troschenkova didn't watch. He didn't want to see the execution. He certainly didn't want to see the look in Vasja's eyes. He heard the report of the handgun, heard the impact of the body on the hard African earth. As the crew began to refuel the jets, another pilot jumped out of the rear of the truck and headed toward him.

"Lieutenant Mikhail Strashnov," he said by way of introduction.

"What's your experience in a Forger?" Troschenkova asked.

"Only about ten hours," Strashnov admitted.

"You're about to double that."

"Yes, sir."

Troschenkova climbed back into his aircraft and powered up. He watched as two of the gunmen dug a hasty grave in the crusty, dried soil. Vasja was gone from the world, but the world would go on without him.

He gave a brief wave to the young pilot in the other Forger and the craft ascended like steel bugs, then accelerated in the direction of the Atlantic Ocean.

The future lay four thousand miles to the northwest.

JUAN ORIOL BOWED his head briefly at the raising of the flag, with its blue and white stripes, a red triangle, a white star. A figure stepped up beside him and touched his arm, and Oriol glanced sideways to identify Joel Perin, a close friend—as close as any friend could get in this line of business, anyway. Perin didn't demand Oriol's attention; he simply wanted Oriol to know he was there. They stood silently as the ceremony continued.

A general was speaking, emphasizing the stellar career of navy General Solas. He called on the ceremony attendees to remember Solas's uncompromising patriotism and loyalty. Oriol didn't remember them. He had never met the man. He wasn't even sure why he was at this function.

Perin had to have been ordered to attend as well, which meant they would probably be paired on whatever assignment arose from Abello's request. Oriol was to report to Abello as soon as the ceremony was completed.

It didn't take long for the eulogy to wrap up.

"Going to headquarters?" Perin asked during the shuffle to leave. He knew Oriol was. There could be no other reason both men were sent to the same event.

"Yes. Meeting with Abello."

"Me, too."

Twenty minutes later they were ushered into the office of General Eduardo Abello of the Cuban secret service. They were silent while the man gave them cigars, a customary courtesy that indicated he was satisfied with their performance for now. They pocketed the cigars and waited patiently in their chairs.

"The man was a traitor," Abello stated abruptly.

"You mean General Solas?" Oriol asked.

"Yes. But I'll guess they didn't mention that during his service."

"No."

"That's because very few people know about it. We know he was bringing drugs into our country and was using his military contacts to deal those drugs on the streets of our cities. He then used the profits for traitorous purposes."

"Can you tell us what purposes?" Perin asked.

"Yes. He's part of an alliance made with many ex-Soviet KGB agents who intend to seize control of the government of Cuba."

"What?" Perin burst out.

"Is there evidence of this?" Oriol asked, dismayed.

"Yes. Divers recovered cocaine from the wreckage of Solas's vessel. The rest was learned through questioning a few close colleagues."

"There are others in the government involved in this?" Oriol suggested.

Abello nodded and leaned forward. "There may be as many as five Cuban military generals involved. Who knows how many of less-important rank?"

"This is unprecedented!" Oriol gasped quietly. "How did this come to light?"

Abello shrugged. "I do not know. I received my information personally and directly from the general of the army and Minister of Revolutionary Armed Forces. He has various intelligence sources, all of which, I imagine, gleaned small bits of information that only formed a full-scale picture when it was brought together on his desk. He contacted me directly because we are old friends—and because he trusts me completely. He knows I am loyal. He knows I will not betray him or the Republic of Cuba.

"In turn, he asked that I call in two trusted to find out more about this traitorous alliance and stop it. That is why you are here."

Oriol and Perin glanced at each other. "General, with a problem of this magnitude, shouldn't there be several agents on the case?"

"There may very well be. The minister does not tell me all his activities. All I know is he wants me to put two men in the field to search out and identify as many of the prime players in this alliance as possible. When they have been identified we will stage simultaneous arrests of the players. In this way he hopes to bring to light all the traitors at one time, giving no one the opportunity to cover their tracks."

"How are we to identify the traitors? Where do we start?"

"By joining their ranks," Abello said simply.

THE SMALL BLACK RUBBER Zodiac raft bounced across the night waves with extraordinarily little sound. The figure at the helm of the Navy SEAL vessel was in a black nylon hooded suit and SEAL gear designed for freedom of movement and nighttime camouflage.

Bolan's face was painted with dark black and green combat cosmetics that would help to hide him on the surface of the water as well as in the dense undergrowth of the island. The commander at Guantánamo had been reluctant to hand out more SEAL equipment after Bolan's destruction of the last raft. Brognola had pulled a few strings, and the SEAL head had become much less argumentative.

The Executioner had parked the *Ocean Missed* far out in the Caribbean. The boat had turned out to be very useful, and he fully appreciated the irony of using the boat against the very people he had stolen it from.

Whoever those people were. Part of his task this night was to confirm what he had learned and determine how to react.

Could there really be an organization of ex-KGB personnel, aided by Cuban and Russian military, intent on taking over Cuba and forming a new Communist regime?

He would know soon. If he found an army waiting for him

on the supposedly abandoned Reunion Island, it would confirm what Mayer had told him.

The truth was, Bolan already believed it. It made sense. It was a picture that the puzzle pieces could fit into.

But he needed to be absolutely sure. No doubts. No hunches. No action based on the questionable reports of unreliable, small-town hoods.

Bolan heard the sound of the surf on the beach ahead of him and cut the engine on the raft, allowing himself to be carried into the island, scanning the foliage with thermal-imaging binoculars. He searched the cool white specters of the palm trees for signs of life but found none.

The DEA reports Brognola had forwarded to him through the computer link at Guantánamo had also reported no activity at Reunion Island. Brognola had wondered about the accuracy of Mayer's report.

"He might have been feeding you a line, Striker," the big Fed said as Bolan scanned the digitized high-resolution aerial photo forming pixel by pixel on his computer screen. The shot was just three weeks old.

"Maybe," Bolan had admitted. "What's that broad area in front of the collapsed house?"

"It's an old helicopter landing pad, according to the report I have."

"Awfully weed-free for having been abandoned two years."

"Yeah," the big Fed admitted after a pause, but doubt was easy to read in his voice. He didn't say that Bolan might be making something out of nothing, but the statement was implied.

"I'll check it out. If it's a waste of time, then it's my loss and nobody else's," Bolan said.

He stepped into the water as it washed onto the sandy beach and dragged the raft onto the shore. The quiet and the darkness were bearing out Brognola's hunch. There had as yet been no tangible sign of an enclave of soldiers-in-training. No sound or light.

But Bolan's gut told him to exercise caution, so he hid the raft in the trees and drew the 93-R as he stalked carefully along the tree line at the edge of the beach.

He found a path of flagstones that led from the beach into the island's interior and started along it, noting that it had been cleared. A hurricane's worth of debris and two years of overgrowth should have crowded it, but the path was open enough for four men to march abreast. It traveled at a gentle curve through the trees, then opened. Bolan stopped when he saw a large, dark space ahead. There was no immediate sign of movement.

As he stepped into the trees, he noted that the soil was hard and crusty in some places, sandy in others, with just enough undergrowth to hide his approach to the collapsed buildings.

Or what appeared to be collapsed buildings.

The roof of what had to have once been a mansion had twisted savagely and fallen in during the onslaught of a long-forgotten hurricane. Recently the roof had been supported from underneath in its broken condition, the rubble cleared from inside and a new shelter placed there. Inside the screened-in barracks were rows and rows of low army cots. Bolan made a quick estimate of three hundred, approximately one-third of which were currently occupied. There wasn't a single flicker of electric light or wood fire anywhere inside the shelter, and the men huddled in wool blankets for warmth in the cool night air.

Antony Mayer's recruits, no doubt.

Bolan wasn't interested in them. They were simply poor young men who had made a bad choice—not that he wouldn't kill them if they attacked and left him no other option.

The soldier waited in his dark corner for fifteen minutes. There would be a guard on duty, probably several, and it was best to know where they were before he made a further reconnaissance.

Bolan had dealt extensively with the KGB and Russian adversaries over the years. There was one element of Russian nature that often gave them away....

All he had to do was wait.

There was a flare of light across the compound. In the pitch blackness it was unmistakable. When the light went out it was replaced by a tiny glowing orange dot. Bolan trained his thermal-imaging binoculars on the spot and made out the corner of a smoker's face from behind a tree.

That was one.

The other made himself known on Bolan's right, next to a storage shed. His efforts to hide the glow of his cigarette in his cupped hands failed. He was a target in the darkness.

Bolan started through the trees again, circling the huge estate and slowing considerably as he came up behind the closest guard. The man was leaning against the storage shed, one hand resting on the butt of the AK-74 slung over his shoulder. He was humming tunelessly, tapping his leg, bored.

The Executioner made his approach under the cover of the humming. Peering in through the wide slats of the shed he saw stacks of packaged bricks of cocaine against one wall. Rows of automatic weapons leaned against another wall.

He spotted boxes of hardware tucked in the darkness. Interesting. He felt the need to know more about it, but first the guard had to go.

He extracted one of the razor-edged stilettos from the rubber-soled, ankle-high shoes he wore and waited for the guard to begin a new song. This time it was Russian pop music, and he sang the words quietly enough that he wouldn't be heard more than a few feet away, but loudly enough to mask the soft sounds of approach the Executioner made.

The stiletto glinted before the guard's eyes, so quickly he didn't understand what he was seeing until his throat was already opened up, the carotid artery and trachea severed. He tried to scream and found he was no longer capable of vocal expression. A split-second later the pain hit him. He felt the earth tilt under his feet and he was lowered to the ground with a stream of wetness flowing out of him. A ghostlike shadow of darkness stood over him in the night. That was the last thing he ever saw.

Bolan dragged the guard into the undergrowth at the edge of the jungle and tucked his AK in the shadows along the side of the building where it wouldn't be noticed. Then he sprinted two steps through the open area to the front entrance of the storage shed.

The door to the ramshackle hut wasn't locked, and he stepped inside with a tiny creak of the wooden hinge. He ignored the guns and the drugs, stepping directly to the rear where he had spotted boxes of unidentifiable electronics. He dragged off the rubber-lined canvas covering and stared at a panel with more than one hundred switches, buttons and toggles, labeled with tiny Cyrillic characters.

Bolan had spent enough time tracking the KGB to have picked up some Russian. Still, it took him a full minute of squinting in the dim moonlight to determine what he was looking at.

It was the remote control for an unmanned Russian bomber aircraft. It was highly sophisticated stuff—despite the plethora of controls offered, the unit could be fed coordinates for anywhere on the planet, align itself via Russian satellite navigation feeds, and target those coordinates with relative accuracy.

It was a good first-strike weapon in the battle to take control of Cuba. A relatively small aircraft might sneak through Cuban air defenses, get directly over Havana and bomb government buildings, sending the government into a state of chaos just prior to the ground attack.

It could even be ordered into kamikaze attacks. Without a pilot to change his resolve at the last minute, the plane could be made to fly directly into a capital building in Havana, packed full of explosives.

Bolan wondered at the irony of protecting the leader of Communist Cuba. But better the old, feeble devil you knew than a new, stronger, more wicked one. He opened the easy-access front panel of the control box and reached into its guts, where he grabbed a handful of wires and extracted them with a forceful yank. Next he groped for the printed circuit boards and an attached set of central processing unit chips. These were the true heart of the control unit, and would be used for remote programming of the unmanned aircraft. Wires could be soldered back in a hurry, but CPUs couldn't be replaced easily. Bolan didn't want to take any chances in allowing this unit to continue to function. He yanked off the printed circuit board and withdrew it, then he used the bloody stiletto to destroy the five tiny computer chips.

There was still the possibility that more than one control unit was in the hands of these men. And they still had the plane. Depending on its configuration, the plane could be programmed internally prior to take off to operate independently. He'd have to destroy that as well.

More arms had to be stored somewhere, on the island or elsewhere, and other bases. And more Russians involved. Bolan needed to know where it all was. He needed a source of information.

A quick survey of the cage revealed no explosives, so the soldier left some of his own. Not enough to shake the island but enough to blast the stash of autorifles into unusable pretzel shapes and burn the cocaine. He planted a small detonator, radio-controlled. The radio operation device was in his pocket, and he would use it if and when a distraction was needed.

So far the probe was soft, and that was how he wanted to keep it.

Back in the cover of the trees he skirted the clearing until he came to what must have been a guest house. It had survived the hurricane better than the main house, and the newcomers had shored up a leaning wall and roof with wooden supports. Bolan guessed that the men in charge housed themselves inside.

The guard was waiting at the opposite corner of the building, meaning Bolan had to circle on the jungle side to come up behind him. His stiletto did its work again, and the guard slumped into Bolan's arms. The soldier dragged the corpse into the weeds, where he would stay unseen as long as it was dark.

A long waiting period revealed no more guards on duty, and Bolan let himself into the guest house by the front door.

He found a sitting room, a dining area and a kitchen on the ground floor. Power had been restored to the building, and the refrigerator rumbled in the corner. Documents were laid out on the dining-area table, and Bolan only glanced at the densely typewritten Cyrillic before shuffling the papers into a single stack and placing them in his pack.

He found the stairs and made his way upward, noticing only a slight tilt to them. The inside of the guest house had survived the hurricane and following two years of abandonment relatively intact, although the carpet gave off a distinct mildew smell.

Upstairs he located three bedrooms, all occupied. He avoided the first, where a man slept with a young black woman curled next to him, and proceeded to the next room, where a single white man was sleeping by himself. He closed the door to the bedroom and switched on the light, leveling the Beretta 93-R as the sleeper came slowly to awareness.

The man's bleary eyes focused on the big handgun and on the giant hovering over his bed. He made an indignant demand in Russian.

"Speak English," Bolan told him, "and speak softly. When is the attack?"

"Who are you?"

"You answer the questions."

"I'll answer nothing. How did you get into this building?"

"I killed two of your guards. You're next."

"I doubt it," a voice said from the doorway.

Bolan crouched and twisted fast, achieving target acquisition on the figure in the door while the words still hung in the air. The 93-R coughed in his hands, and the half-dressed Russian fired an instant later. The man's aim was high and off, while the 9 mm parabellum round slammed directly into the center of his chest as if computer-aimed. The Russian staggered back into the hall and crashed into the wall, slumping to the ground, his handgun rattling to the floor.

The man in the bed had used the diversion to grab at something under his pillow and Bolan turned on him next, firing as the Russian withdrew a snub-nosed pistol. The bullet, fired from a low angle, entered under his rib cage and ripped through his heart and lungs before crashing into his shoulder blade. The Russian collapsed on the mattress.

There was one more Russian on the third floor—not to mention his islander girlfriend—and Bolan operated under the assumption they were fully aware of what was going on. He stepped to the door and looked for movement. There was none, but there was a shuffle of sound from the next bedroom that he knew was generated by people moving and trying to be quiet about it. They would have the hallway covered.

Stepping across the bedroom he opened the door to the balcony. It was narrow and small but extended alongside the building. Chances were good the inhabitants of the next room would be watching that egress as well, but it was his only quick-attack option. He stepped onto the balcony silently, moving to the French doors of the next bedroom and peering through the lace window covering, ready to dodge a bullet.

The light from the bedroom he had just left made the figures guarding the bedroom door a silhouette and showed plainly that they were neglecting the balcony doors. Bolan aimed through the glass and the curtains, which he knew would have little effect on the path of the 9 mm bullet, and fired one time.

The woman screamed and collapsed to the floor, hands over her head. The Russian twisted in a half circle and reached for the doorjamb, eyes wide, handgun bouncing on the carpet at his feet. He stared at the ceiling in surprise and grabbed at the bloody crater in his left hip.

Bolan pushed at the French doors and stepped inside. The 93-R didn't waver from his Russian target, who stared at him with the wide eyes of near shock. Bolan had to get answers from the man soon, before the man became incoherent.

"Who are you?"

"Serghej Samodurov, Soviet KGB," he articulated painstakingly.

"There's no more KGB and there's no more Soviet Union."

"There will be a new Union and it will be the legacy of the KGB," Samodurov declared with great effort, his brow covered with sweat. He turned to lean against the doorjamb and slid slowly to the floor.

"When will the attack occur?"

"Even if I gave you that information you couldn't stop it."

"Then tell me."

"I'll tell you nothing. The New Revolution is at hand—"

Samodurov nodded his head to his chest. He wasn't going to be answering any further questions.

The woman had stopped sobbing as she watched her lover die. Her face was stamped with bewilderment, but when she looked up at Bolan it turned to terror.

"Are you from Barry Bay?"

The woman nodded.

"I need to know who these men are and everything they have planned to do. Can you tell me anything? I need files, papers, computers, notes, diaries, anything. Do you know where they would be?"

She nodded. Bolan gestured with the gun and she got to her feet and had to visibly summon the courage to step over Samodurov's corpse. She went to the hall, keeping an eye on Bolan over her shoulder as if she thought he would shoot her in the back the moment she wasn't looking.

She led him back to the last bedroom and opened a set of wide closet doors. Inside was a desk and a small laptop. Bolan grabbed it and tucked it into his pack, along with the single box of floppy disks sitting open next to it. The desk drawers contained nothing else that looked as if it might be useful.

"Where are the rest of the Russians?" he demanded.

The woman summoned the courage to speak for the first time. "They have tents in the trees—that way, behind the house."

"Go to the tents. Wake all the island men and tell them to get down to the water on the north side of the island. Tell them to stay away from the Russians and away from all the weapons. Understand?''

The young woman nodded.

''If they associate with the Russians they might get killed, because I might kill them. Got it?''

She nodded, and he could see she believed his words.

He flung the pack on his back, and they descended to the front door of the guest house. The night was still, but Bolan knew the sound of the gunfire from the Russian's weapon would probably have alerted the Russians in their tents if they were nearby. He would operate under the assumption that they were on the prowl even now.

''You walk across the compound swiftly and quietly. If they try to stop you, tell them you saw me running in the other direction. Then get your men up.''

The young woman nodded and started across the compound with a brisk step. She wasn't challenged. If there were men who saw her, they didn't make themselves known.

Bolan crossed the dangerous, moon-lighted zone in front of the building just as she disappeared into the pavilion barracks. He slipped into the weeds, heading away from the guest house, in search of tents housing Russian soldiers.

He stopped when he heard a harsh whisper in the darkness, drawing his Ka-bar fighting knife from its sheath. Even the suppressed 93-R was probably too noisy for a close encounter in the woods with unknown assailants nearby. But the combat knife killed in silence. The blade was as black as the night, anodized except along the freshly sharpened edge.

He approached a heavy palm tree and glimpsed a figure on the other side, staring away from him, an AK at the ready in his hands. His head turned as if he heard something far off to the right, then he looked to the left, never realizing that death came from the rear.

Bolan's hand snaked around the palm tree trunk and sliced the blade neatly across the gunman's throat, then he stepped around the tree, grabbing the AK as it fell from his victim's grip and pressed the barrel into the dying man's gut, just under his rib cage. He lowered the corpse to the ground, arranging the AK-74 hastily to make it look as though the man was simply sitting down on the job—at least from a distance. Bolan stepped into the trees again, searching for more Russians.

The hiss heard minutes before had been between two people, which meant others were awake, alert, on the prowl.

Another hiss. Another Russian. Bolan halted, curving his body to match the slope of the tree trunk he used as cover, watching for the infinitesimally minute shifts in the dark forest shadows that indicated men were about.

The undergrowth was growing thinner, the soil sandier. The Russian tents had to be on or near the beach. Bolan was doubly watchful, knowing how easily even untrained men might stalk prey silently on sandy soil.

There it was, the shift he was looking for, the movement of one tiny speck of dark shadow among the rest of the shadows, incongruous in the still night, Bolan would have been hard-pressed to say exactly what he saw or where he saw it specifically.

He just knew.

He stepped out from the palm tree with the 93-R leveled and squeezed the trigger during the quarter of a second it took him to locate and evaluate his target. The Russian spotted him and swung in his direction, but he'd already heard the cough of the weapon.

The round took the Russian in the chest and gave him a shove. He threw the AK away as if he were suddenly fed up with it, and it struck the sand muzzle-first. The Russian inhaled raggedly, then collapsed where he stood.

Bolan grabbed the AK-74 from the sand, leveled it into the soil and triggered it once, twice, then a final time, laying on the trigger until the magazine suddenly ran dry. The sound of the gunfire filled the island from end to end.

He backed into the nearest bush for cover.

The Russians came shouting through the trees. Bolan sighted on the open spot where he was sure some of them would emerge, then squeezed the trigger at the first man to barrel out, armed with a Kalashnikov autorifle. The 9 mm parabellum round slammed into his skull, a perfect head shot that knocked him dead instantly. The gunman directly behind him had to sidestep quickly to avoid the toppling corpse. He looked at his comrade for just two seconds before realizing it was just a corpse, then sought wildly for the killer. He never heard the sound of the next round from the 93-R. It slammed into his forehead and killed him where he stood.

Two more men emerged from another location and entered the scene from Bolan's right. He shifted his shooter's stance and didn't bother to be quiet about it. One of the men glanced at the corpses, then looked directly at him. Maybe he had jungle training. Maybe he was simply extraordinarily perceptive. He started to shout and the next 9 mm round punched into his pectoral, knocking him to the sand. His companion began running and Bolan targeted the blur that was his legs, firing a pair of rounds that sent the other man to the ground. Both men were on the sand, moaning in pain.

Bolan heard no one else on the approach and stepped into the open. He saw the second gunner attempt to bring his AK into firing position, but didn't allow him to use it. A single suppressed subsonic round drilled through the bridge of his nose, ending the threat.

The first wounded man had somehow managed to drag himself on his hands to his AK. Spread-eagle on his back, his wounded chest crusted with sand, he weakly raised the AK in Bolan's direction, wavering drunkenly. The Executioner dropped to his knees, and the autofire ripped into the air above him. The soldier fired under its canopy, triggering three rounds into the firing hand, knocking the AK askew so that errant rounds wouldn't slice him in two. He directed a bullet into the flat, helpless Russian, who curled over the fresh wound as if he were a bug and the 9 mm round, the pin that impaled him.

Bolan froze and listened.

He heard distant voices, confusion and activity. The woman was raising the recruits as he'd ordered. He hoped none of them tried anything stupid. They were simply poverty-stricken, exploited people. But if Bolan was attacked by one of them, he would, of course, defend himself.

A quick head count of the Russian dead came to eleven. Would they keep a contingent that small on the island?

Perhaps.

He turned and continued into the trees, within several paces coming to two large tents placed together so they could see out into the small northern bay. He looked inside each of the tents and found them empty.

If there were more Russians, they were in hiding. Bolan wasn't about to scour the island. He had more important things to accomplish.

THE OPEN AREAS of the island were filled with the Jamaican recruits, milling without order or purpose.

"They won't go to the north end," the young woman said, approaching Bolan as he stepped into the open.

"It doesn't matter," Bolan replied. "I think all the Russians are dead."

The men began to group around him, anxious to know what was going on.

"You kill all these Russian guys?" one man demanded.

"Yeah."

"Why'd you do that, man?"

Bolan found himself staring eye-to-eye with a huge, brawny islander, marked by bloodshot eyes and a wrinkled brow.

"They had evil intent," Bolan said quietly.

The islander didn't seem to know what to make of that. Bolan pushed past him and headed to the trees.

"Wait a minute! What are we supposed to do?" the young woman asked.

"Do whatever you want. But I suggest you stay away from that shed," Bolan replied, holstering the Beretta and reaching into his shirt pocket.

"Why?" she persisted.

The shed exploded in a ball of fire that sent the islanders scrambling in the other direction.

By the time they overcame their shock, the Executioner had disappeared.

6

"There is something very strange going on with our Russian friends," Brognola said over the phone line.

"Explain," Bolan demanded.

"They haven't admitted anything officially, of course. But there have been reports of increasing frequencies of thefts among the Russian military. Not minor thefts, either. Big stuff, Striker."

"How big?"

"Yesterday they lost a couple Yak Forger VTOLs."

That was big. A vertical take-off/landing strike fighter was a substantial piece of offensive equipment. "You wouldn't think they'd leave the keys in it."

"They didn't. In fact evidence points to heightened security throughout all levels of the Russian military in recent weeks. Still, somehow, they lost the planes. They came off the *Admiral Kuznetsov*, which is cruising off the west coast of Africa. Our reports indicate the two Forgers left on what was thought to be an authorized mission—fully armed, not just maneuvers—and didn't come back. Now nobody knows where they are. Although the USAF reports getting a fix on two Russian jets over the Atlantic late last night."

"Heading due west," Bolan added.

"You've got it, more or less."

"Any further reports—like where they might have put down?"

"They're VTOLs so they could put down anywhere on the planet. No, to answer your question."

"I think they were scheduled to make a stop or even a permanent base at Reunion Island, the one you thought was abandoned. Well, there used to be a major contingent of our Russians guys stationed there, training their Jamaican recruits."

"Used to be? Where did they go?"

"I paid a visit to them last night," Bolan explained. "The guys in charge were Russians. Now they're out of the play. I sent their recruits back to Jamaica to look for less hazardous employment. I found some interesting items on the island, however. One was a control unit for an unmanned Russian bomber aircraft, which I bet is one of the pieces of hardware recently burgled from the Russian military."

Brognola exhaled. "That would be a pretty useful item in their Cuban offensive."

"Well, the box is no longer useful to anyone. It's scrap metal now, as is the Soviet weaponry they had on hand. I didn't find the plane that the box controlled, but I did remove a notebook computer and some disks from one of the Russians. As soon as we're through talking, I'll plug it in to the Farm and you can let Bear nose around to see what can be found that'll help me at this end."

"Right. Kurtzman will love it," the big Fed said.

BOLAN PLUGGED the laptop into the telephone wall socket in his hotel room, easily establishing a link with Stony Man Farm. The Farm was equipped with a T1 connection—several of them, actually—but Bolan had to make do with the 28,800-baud modem purchased at a small electronics shop in Montego Bay. The load took several hours, but the members of the Farm team began to translate downloaded files as soon as they had them in their hands.

"Most of it's garbage and we're not even bothering to translate it. There's also a substantial amount of material downloaded from the *alt.anarchy* and *alt.chaos.communist* Internet newsgroups. Interesting reading but not exactly pertinent," Brognola said.

"The on-line groups supposedly get access to some clandestine information, especially the shortwave-radio enthusiasts," Bolan commented, "or so I hear. Maybe they were monitoring the Internet groups to see how much the world knows about the thefts from the Russian government."

"For what purpose?"

"Stands to reason that if the newsgroups know, then Castro knows," Bolan said. "That could have an effect on what the outlaw KGBers make use of and when."

Brognola was quiet for a moment. "You're right. We'll start going through those downloads more carefully. But we've also uncovered some information you'll find immediately useful. We're translating it as fast as we can, and we'll have most of it ready to send back to you—well, right now."

"Anything else?"

"Yeah." Brognola's voice was hushed. "I've been in touch with the President, Striker. He's not a nervous guy, but I think this situation has him a little edgy."

"He should be."

"He can't do anything about this. He can't even warn Castro. Hell, he'd probably do cartwheels if somebody ousted Castro—anybody except the guys who might actually do it. If he sends anybody to intervene officially, Cuba will see it as an act of aggression and you know what that would do for relations.

"But most of all, he can't allow a bunch of power-hungry, well-armed, well-trained extremists take over. It would be a Cuban Missile Crisis all over again. It would put a hostile nation with potential nuclear capability within close proximity of U.S. shores. He couldn't allow that to happen. He'd have to strike back, and the result might be full-fledged war. Thank God you haven't found evidence of nuclear capability among these KGBers yet."

"I haven't exactly performed a thorough search, either."

"I know that—"

"And nobody has a clear picture of the location of all the radioactive material and devices that once belonged to the Soviet Union. German magazine reporters have been buying Soviet radioactive material just to prove how easy it is. If a German writer can buy a nuclear weapon, I think it's a safe bet that a well-connected group of former KGB and Soviet military insiders have access to them. If they don't already have a couple nuclear devices sitting in their houseboats as we speak. You ought to make sure the Man knows that.''

"I will, Striker.''

Bolan hung up the phone and unplugged it, reconnecting the modem and reestablishing his Stony Man link. At once the translated documents began downloading onto the hard drive.

They made for very interesting reading, indeed.

BOLAN DIDN'T HAVE ACCESS to a printer. But he desired only to write down a few names and a few details. They went into his war book, a small, leather-bound notebook he carried with him at all times. In it, among other things, were the names of many men who had made themselves the Executioner's targets in years past. Nearly all of those men were now dead.

It also contained the names of people Bolan wished to investigate when he had the time and the inclination.

The names in the translated Russian documents were all unfamiliar, except one: Manuel Quinones, the cartel head Bolan had targeted when he first stumbled across the Russians in Haiti. Now his name was refreshed in the soldier's mind.

The extent of the Quinones-KGB connection wasn't spelled out in the documents, but there was enough for Bolan to act on.

A short communiqué provided by the U.S. Drug Enforcement Administration (USDEA) via Aaron Kurtzman appeared on the hard drive just before the link was severed. That gave Bolan an even more precise target.

His course of action was clear.

JIMMY CIE STROLLED out of the police station rolling his shoulders, feeling tired, feeling disillusioned. He tried to do some good, but there were always so many wrong paths for people to take. The best he could do, it seemed, was to pick up the pieces. He wished there was some way for him to steer people away from those wrong paths before they started down them, to give people fewer options for evil so less evil would be committed. Or something like that.

He sat in his car and tried to fine-tune the radio station but failed. He never even noticed the man until he stood like a ghost at his shoulder.

"Evening, Detective."

"WHERE DID YOU GET this information?" Cie asked, as they watched the small apartment building from the street.

"I managed to get access to the personal computer files of one of their top men. It gave me a list of several of their locations and activities throughout the Western Hemisphere."

"Very useful. How did you manage to persuade the man who had this information to give it up?"

"He was in no position to argue."

Cie looked at him sideways and shook his head.

"You're a cold man, Belasko."

"You're right, Detective."

"Now, what do you mean by Western Hemisphere? You mean they have guys operating outside Jamaica?"

Bolan nodded. "Yucatán. Hispaniola. Guatemala. The list goes on. They're experienced, and they have connections. They know well enough not to concentrate their resources in one location. You never know when that location might be compromised. Like the Reunion Island base. They had a lot of Jamaican manpower there, but not all that much in terms of hardware or investment, or their own staff. The loss of those Russians and the hardware will slow them down, but not by much. They still have hardware all over the Caribbean, and their own staff at all those locations."

"So what's your role in this, Belasko? What're you going to try to do about it?"

"Take them down."

"Here in Jamaica?"

"Everywhere."

Cie considered that. "By yourself?"

"If I have to. But you're helping me."

"I'm a Jamaican detective. I'm not going to Guatemala with you, Belasko. I'm not even going to Hispaniola."

"I'm not asking you to. I'll take care of those facilities myself."

"You're confident that you can take down this group all on your own, aren't you, man?"

Bolan said nothing, watching the apartment building, where a figure walked past the window behind the curtains. He had located the names of the two bases of operations in Jamaica: the arms storage and recruitment location in Barry Bay, now defunct, and a two-flat building in Montego Bay that had been completely rented by the Russians. Bolan didn't know who the players were at the Montego Bay base. He might have wiped out most of them when he took out the soldiers at Barry Bay. But before he moved on to new theaters of the conflict he'd make sure he beat all the rats from the Jamaican nests.

Jimmy Cie's assistance had been invaluable. He could nose around without arousing suspicion. Bolan had placed a call to him as soon as he'd disengaged from Stony Man Farm and asked him to find out what he could about the Montego Bay address. Questioning the landlord turned up useful information: there had been as many as eight Europeans living in the building at one time. In the past day that number had shrunk to four. They also kept a contingent of four locals. "Bad men. Hoods," the landlord told Cie.

Twenty minutes of stakeout had revealed to them there were at least seven men in the building. Bolan was hoping to catch all the players at home, but he was getting itchy. Sitting in a car like a big-city detective on a stakeout wasn't his style.

He got lucky. A white man pulled up in a rented Scirocco and parked in front of the house. Bolan and Cie listened intently as he knocked on the door to the flat. There had to have been a call from inside, because the white man responded to it.

He answered in Russian. The door was opened and he disappeared inside.

"That's eight to two, Belasko."

"No one's asking you to come with me."

Cie shrugged. "Might as well," he said, pulling his Browning Hi-Power from its holster and checking the magazine.

"You're welcome to make use of some of my hardware," Bolan said, nodding toward the back seat, where he had flung his overstuffed canvas bag. He grabbed it and opened it, eliciting a whistle from Cie.

"Heavy duty."

"You know how to use this?" Bolan asked, handing him a piece of equipment.

"I've fired something like it."

"It's a Heckler & Koch MP-5. Very effective in close confrontations, and it could get tight in there. It fires a 9 mm round and has a 30-round magazine. Here." He handed Cie two more of the curved magazines. "You've got ninety rounds. But they'll go fast if you can't control the weapon."

"Got it."

Bolan grabbed his own equipment, and they left Cie's vehicle.

MAX CANAAN WAS READING one of the Miami newspapers the Russians subscribed to. He had no idea why they would be interested in the goings-on in the U.S. He wasn't all that interested himself, but he had nothing else to do so he intended to read it, front page to last. There was a knock.

"Yeah?"

"Open the door," Bolan said in Russian, well enough to fool someone who didn't speak the language.

Canaan had thought all the Russians were in the building, but one of them had to have left again when he wasn't aware of it. Or maybe they had other Russians coming to visit them.

It never occurred to him that a newcomer who could speak Russian might be an enemy.

He opened the door.

Two men were standing there, one a white man, the other black.

"Who are you?" Canaan asked.

"Let us in, man," the black guy said with obvious irritation.

"Not until I know who you are," Canaan answered.

The white guy moved fast, snatching at a holster under his dark, safari jacket, and Canaan saw the flash of a handgun. He grabbed for his own piece, yanking it out of the holster, which he never kept snapped, and simultaneously stepping sideways to draw himself out of the line of fire. But he witnessed the white man step into the doorway, level the gun and trigger it, all so fast Canaan never had a chance to use his own weapon. He tried to shout but the single round from the handgun entered his body and flung him back. He didn't know if he made a sound or not. Then his consciousness turned out like a light.

Bolan regretted that the man managed to shout before he hit the wall with a thud and thumped to the floor. So much for a stealthy probe. There was a call from the living room to the left and Bolan stepped to the corner, searching for his target. Another black guard spotted him first and dived through a far door.

"Intruders!" he shouted. He reappeared in the doorway leveling an AK-74, but Bolan had been waiting for a first site of him and triggered the Beretta 93-R, sending a round crashing into the guard the moment he appeared. The guard flopped out of sight.

Two down, at least six to go. And now the alarm had been raised.

Bolan swept the living room and followed the downed guard through the rear doorway, finding himself in a small eating area. There was a curse from the left, from what he assumed was a bedroom. The soldier hopped over the body, avoiding the blood, and stepped into the narrow apartment kitchen, which was empty. He peered around the wall toward the bedroom. A head poked from the bedroom door, but the man wasn't looking in Bolan's direction.

The figure that stepped out had messed hair and wore only a pair of slacks. The probe had woken him and he wasn't thinking clearly yet, but he held a Colt automatic handgun in a two-handed grip. He kept his gaze glued on the opening into the living room, wasting no more than a glance on the dead guard. He took three steps, fully exposed, before Bolan made his move, stepping out of the kitchen and aiming the 93-R— at the same instant a woman emerged from the bedroom.

"Sergei!" she cried. Bolan didn't allow himself to be distracted—it might cost him his life. The Russian man whipped the Colt into target acquisition, but the Executioner was already firing. The 9 mm parabellum round cut into the Russian's stomach. Bolan turned the gun on the doorway just in time to see the woman bring her own snub-nosed Smith & Wesson into play. She fired prematurely, sending a round into the floor to Bolan's left, but the soldier didn't allow himself to make such a mistake. The suppressed round slammed into her chest just below the collarbone, sending her flying into the bedroom on her back. Bolan whipped the 93-R back to the collapsing gunman, firing an insurance round into his skull.

With three fast paces he chased the woman into the bedroom, where he found her on her back, staring at the ceiling in an openmouthed grimace. No second glance was needed to convince him the room was empty.

Shots sounded from the second floor.

CIE LEAPED UP the first flight of stairs in three long strides and twisted on the landing, facing the next flight with his back landing heavily against the wall. The door at the top of the stairs burst open, and a Russian emerged with a Jamaican right behind him. Both looked surprised and raised their weapons when they saw an intruder waiting for them. Cie pressed the butt of the MP-5 into his ribs and triggered the weapon, 9 mm rounds bursting from the muzzle and crashing into the wooden steps. He adjusted his aim quickly, and the trail of destruction ate its way into the two men, who shook one after another in a rag-doll dance before collapsing on the landing.

Cie advanced up the next flight of stairs, keeping the door to the upper flat covered. There was a flash of movement and a guard appeared in the doorway, already in a perfect firing stance, as if he had been teleported there instantly. Cie squeezed the trigger and a half-dozen 9 mm rounds crunched into the gunman, flinging him out of the doorway, his handgun firing into the ceiling.

Automatic rifle fire originated from inside somewhere and chopped at the doorframe, the wall and the ceiling. The detective crouched on the stairs and waited for the barrage to halt, trying to put a number on the rounds he had fired. It was easy to expel an entire mag from the MP-5 without even realizing it. He couldn't chance it. He snatched off the old mag and clicked in another.

A rush of footsteps behind him drew Cie's attention, and he directed the subgun at the approaching figure.

Bolan saw the weapon swing in his direction, then move away.

"Downstairs is clear. I got four of them."

"Two more dead on the landing," Cie said.

"We can't count on our estimate of eight men," Bolan stated. "There could very well be more we don't know about. Take care."

Cie nodded as the soldier came to the steps behind him. The upstairs flat was quiet. Bolan raised his head to the level of the floor. Behind the corpses he saw an empty section of the flat. No sign of life.

He gestured as he holstered the 93-R and drew the Remington 870. The 12-gauge combat shotgun was mounted on a swing-out sling under his right shoulder. The weapon was the right choice for a close-contact encounter with an unknown number of assailants.

Bolan and Cie achieved the landing. The door to the flat was open ninety degrees, and they could see a furnished living room. No one was visible, but there were at least two people inside, at least one with an automatic weapon.

They could be anywhere, including directly behind the door.

The Executioner pointed to Cie and gestured that he should take the right side of the room. Bolan would take the left. He placed himself slightly in front of Cie, then stepped inside, shouldering the door with a body blow designed to knock a man off his feet if he was stationed behind it. The door crashed into the wall, and when Bolan spotted a white man behind a large television with an AK-74, he triggered the Remington. The 12-gauge shot shattered the television screen with sudden music and shredded the gunner's chest and face. The AK never fired.

Cie spotted a Jamaican with a 9 mm Browning BDA autopistol behind a counter that defined the kitchen and he triggered the MP-5, cutting a deadly 9 mm swathe across the gunman at chest level. The BDA clattered onto the carpet and the gunman cracked his head on the refrigerator as he collapsed.

Bolan whirled to render assistance in time to witness the gunman's collapse and to see another white man triggering an autorifle from the darkness of an unlit hallway. He heard Cie cry out, but had to ignore it for now. He pumped the shotgun and triggered it into the hall. The close-proximity blast was devastating, ripping the wall into plaster snow and ripping the gunman to shredded meat from head to toe, flinging him into the back of the hall as if tossed by a gigantic wind.

The Executioner kicked at the bedroom doors and found both rooms empty. He returned to the living room in a hurry.

Too late to be of any good.

Jimmy Cie was dead.

On the streets of Montego Bay, dusk was encroaching.

7

Juan Oriol left the office just after 5:00 p.m. but didn't return home. Instead he circled the block and parked. He walked along the side street and came to a small hotel used often by visiting dignitaries. It was an elegant place, very expensive, the best place to stage his watch.

He watched for two hours.

It was nearing eight before he spotted the last light go off in the offices of Cuban army General Javier Serra, where Oriol had been working for the past three days as an assistant to the general. Only today had he managed to get access to a key to the private files the general kept. Tonight he intended to make use of that key.

The last figure to leave the office was the general himself. Minutes after the lights went off, Oriol spotted the gates to the courtyard lot open and the general pull out in his Mercedes. The guard at the gate gave him a wave and the vehicle continued on into the city of Havana.

It was time for Oriol's probe. He left the hotel, found his car and reentered the Cuban army offices building. His DGA-supplied paperwork identified him as an army captain with authorization to enter the building. The guards gave him no trouble.

He rode the creaking elevator to the fifth floor and took the stairs to the sixth. The floor looked deserted; the lights were off. He stepped into the hall and held the door so that it would shut silently.

Oriol strode quickly to the general's office and unlocked the outer doors. The inner offices had the quiet, cool feel of evening.

He locked the doors behind him and strode to the general's private office. He put his hand against it and listened again, but heard nothing. He unlocked the heavy oak door.

The room was in darkness, and a light from the hotel sign across the street emitted a warm glow. Oriol crossed the carpet and lowered the blinds, sealing himself in blackness that would have been utter if not for the tiny red dot from a ceiling-mounted smoke detector. Only then did he turn on the desk lamp.

He tried his plastic replica key in the general's private file drawer, which opened with a click.

He pulled open the drawer and sat in the general's leather chair, leafing through the file tags. There weren't many, and none aroused his interest. Oriol began to remove files and riffle through their contents: progress reports and the general's personnel evaluations; top-secret reports from other generals on national security issues. None of it seemed suspicious.

Oriol returned the files to the drawer and sat there for a moment, wondering what to do next. He opened all the drawers, searching for a false bottom. He found a half-consumed fifth of Cuban rum and a Spanish-made pistol under a sheath of papers. Nothing incriminating.

The infiltration wouldn't be a total waste—he carefully planted a wireless bug under the lip of the desk.

Closing up everything and locking the file drawer the way he had found it, Oriol turned off the desk lamp and raised the blinds to the height they had been when he entered. He left the general's office, almost on tiptoe.

He didn't know that the tiny video camera, hidden inside the functional fire alarm in the ceiling, recorded every move he made.

THE FOUR-SEATER helicopter hovered over the island in the darkness, waiting for a signal.

"I told you there was something wrong! I knew it was more than just busted radios!"

"Shut up," Guryanov snarled. Shishkin gave him a hang-dog look and shut up.

"Well," Guryanov said finally, "there's nothing for it but to go in."

"Go in? What if there's an ambush waiting for us?" Shishkin asked in alarm.

"Then keep your head down." Guryanov was learning to despise Shishkin, who was a ball-less wonder. How had a mouse like him ever risen in the ranks of the KGB?

"Down!" Guryanov ordered their pilot. He nodded, and the helicopter began to descend smoothly onto the paved area. The searchlights swept over the first of the corpses when the aircraft was still five yards from the ground.

"There!" Guryanov said, thrusting his finger at it. The pilot spun the chopper so that the searchlight stabbed at the fallen man, clearly a Russian, clearly quite dead, lying next to the guest house that had served as the Russian's living quarters on the island.

The aircraft touched the bricks and the rotors spun down quickly.

"Keep this thing in a state of readiness," Shishkin barked. "Be ready to take off on a moment's notice."

"Yes, sir."

Guryanov was already getting out, with a flashlight in one hand and his long-trusted Tokarev handgun in the other. Shishkin followed with the autorifle he had insisted on bringing.

Guryanov hurried to the body. The rush of air from the landing helicopter had disturbed the flies for a moment, but they were flooding back over the man, crawling in and around the wound that had killed him and in and out of his open mouth and nostrils.

"Sweet mother!" Shishkin exclaimed.

Guryanov shone his flashlight across the compound onto the makeshift pavilion, where one hundred Jamaican mercenary recruits should have been housed. Obviously nobody was home now. Not far from the pavilion was the gated shed where the Russians had stored some of their hard-won equipment. Nothing was left of the shed now but charred bits of wood and bent, twisted black shapes that had once been AK-74s. The auto-plane control was demolished. Of the cocaine there was no trace.

The Russian stomped across the open area again to the guest house. He tried the light switches and nothing happened. The generator had either been destroyed or simply not refueled.

He didn't need the lights. His flashlights found the corpses well enough. There were fewer flies inside, but somehow the silent, staring dead men seemed even more horrible in the darkness, as if they weren't dead but simply frozen in time—a time Guryanov wanted no part of.

Shishkin maintained a steady dialogue with himself as they moved from body to body. They quickly identified all the dead men. Every Russian was present and accounted for, every one of them dead.

"You think the mercs revolted?" Shishkin asked.

"Look around you. No dead Jamaicans."

"You don't think there was infighting?"

"No, I do not."

"What happened, then? These men weren't killed by ghosts. Unless ghosts carry guns."

"Whoever it was obviously outgunned our men, then simply took their own dead away with them. They outgunned the Jamaicans too, if the Jamaicans even involved themselves. The surviving Jamaicans took the boats and went home. What else were they supposed to do?"

"Who, though?" Shishkin asked. "Who could have known about us?"

"Whoever the Jamaicans told. Whoever it was who took out our men in Barry Bay."

"Cubans?"

"I don't know, Andrei," Guryanov said impatiently, and his flashlight beam played over the face of a dead man. His eyes were open, staring unwavering into space, his hands frozen as they clawed at the massive wound in his chest. "But I have a feeling we will found out eventually."

BOLAN WAS STEERING the *Ocean Missed* out of the Montego Bay harbor even while city police were responding to the reports of gunfire. A quick phone call to Virginia had laid the groundwork for the next stage.

"All I need is an airlift and no questions," he explained quickly. "No matter how careful the Man is being he can't think a simple airlift is going to get the U.S. in any trouble. No one will even know."

"Agreed," Brognola stated. He had said he would be in contact with Guantánamo within minutes.

Bolan hoped so, because he wasn't waiting around Montego Bay to get an answer.

The drug smugglers' boat had served him well and he hated to abandon it. On the other hand, he needed fast transport to the Yucatán Peninsula, almost eight hundred miles away. The *Ocean Missed* would take forever.

The CH-46 Sea Knight assault helicopter would make the trip in somewhat less time.

The radio signal came in just after midnight, and Bolan waved to the six-ton helicopter from the top deck. The chopper descended upon him like a behemoth from a monster movie, its twin rotors roaring like sibling hurricanes, rocking the vessel and spraying away the calm Caribbean water in huge clouds. The helmeted crewman gave Bolan a short wave and dropped the ladder, which unrolled during its descent and stopped within inches of Bolan's head. He hoisted on his pack and grabbed the ladder. Seconds later he was climbing inside the Sea Knight as it ascended and veered due west.

"What about your boat?" the crewman asked.

"You want it?"

LULLED BY THE STEADY thrum of the twin rotors, Bolan managed to get some much-needed shut-eye, but soon enough the crewman was shaking him awake and offering him a cup of broth. Bolan downed it and ate several cold rations. He had no idea when he would have the chance to stop for a meal again.

"We'll be at your coordinates in twenty minutes," the crewman offered. "Maybe I should show you how to use some of this stuff."

"I don't think that'll be necessary," Bolan replied and began to check his gear. He had instructed Brognola to get him a shopping list of heavy-duty SEAL-issue gear. He had an M-88 for long-range shooting, rappel gear, rations, a canteen and a tool kit. His final addition was an M-16 A-1/M-203.

The crewman brought out the parachute harness. Bolan took one look at it and shook his head. "Give me the MT1XS rig," he said. "I'll need the air time to scout the terrain."

The crewman decided against arguing. He replaced the smaller MC1-1B chute on its mount and grabbed the rig for the MT1XS. The larger rig was designed for heavy, high-altitude jumps, and with 370 feet of chute it could accommodate a man as big as Bolan plus an extra 100 pounds of gear. Bolan wasn't jumping with that much gear, so the slow descent of the MT1XS would give him time to get the lay of the land.

The crewman looked nervous, but he didn't say anything. His orders were to get their guest ready to jump—giving him unquestioned cooperation—and then forget he ever existed. The kid was sure hoping the big man knew what he was doing. SEALs typically trained for long, hard months before being allowed anywhere near this type of equipment.

The crewman received a message from the cockpit and tilted his head to get it better. "Affirmative on that." He turned to Bolan. "We're at your coordinates, sir. Is there anything else you need?"

"No, thanks," Bolan said as the rear doors of the CH-46 opened up with a rush of warm, humid air. He gave the crewman a wave and walked into open space.

The air came alive around him as he rushed headlong away from the Sea Knight, already turning and heading east.

Bolan forgot the helicopter as he took in the moonlit expanse of Guatemala spread out beneath him. It took him two seconds, no more, to get a fix on his location, and as the huge parachute unfurled he brought himself into a north-facing position. Ahead of him by several miles was the mountain he was looking for, called Cayos. Looking down and between his legs, he spotted a sliver of river, shining like the scrap of a moon the day after it rises new. Between Cayos Mountain and the river, and off to Bolan's left, was the tiny Guatemalan town of Carapito. Northeast, hidden in the jungles, was a compound called Little Hell.

This was one of the homes and training grounds for a band of mercenary soldiers that went by the colorful name Soldiers of Hell. They had been given the English name by their two founders, Gary Albrecht and Brian Fagen. The men were ex-U.S. Marines, both highly decorated and both with reputations for ignoring the rules. They left the armed forces together in the late 1980s and were known to have circulated among various militia groups. In 1993, fed up with what they saw as Big Brother government in the United States—a government that had grown no better with the coming to power of a Democrat president—they left the U.S. altogether. The CIA took an interest in the two when they began operating as mercenaries in the Belize-Mexican-Guatemalan corner of the Yucatán Peninsula. The band of mercs that eventually built itself around the two men made good use of the three borders, crossing and recrossing as was convenient, never settling long in their various bases.

A few miles outside Carapito they had forged what was known to be a permanent base, more or less, and training facility. During the revolts by the Mexican Indian tribes in 1994, the U.S. had homed its satellites on the Carapito base and developed a map of the facility before deciding there was nothing untoward happening at the base that required the attention of the Central Intelligence Agency.

A GIF version of the map had been among the information Aaron Kurtzman fed Bolan over the stolen laptop. The soldier had memorized the layout of Little Hell like it was his own backyard.

The files translated from the laptop had clearly indicated that the ex-KGB team had purchased full cooperation from the soldiers. They were using the men, using the Carapito compound for training men, using their hardware. The soldiers had essentially joined the Russians' cause.

Which meant the soldiers had signed themselves on as enemies of the free world.

Guatemala was warm, peaceful and quiet when one was floating over it at three thousand feet in the middle of the night. But soon the sun would rise, the day would get hot and that peace would be shattered into a thousand bloody pieces.

BOLAN FOUND A CLEARING in the jungle and dropped into it at a run, twisting the chute into a ball and stuffing it, along with the harness, into the leaves of a twisted, low bush without pausing to slow down. Seconds later he was marching through the undergrowth in the direction of Little Hell.

By dawn he was in a tree that looked out over the wide field that had been chosen for the facility. Bolan counted five buildings, in addition to two guard towers. There was a fuel dump, a roofed area to keep vehicles out of the sun and a single Russian Yak Forger VTOL strike fighter, parked and camouflaged.

The rising sun brought the inhabitants to life. A bugle call summoned the men for inspection. Bolan found the inspection most beneficial, indeed. It told him how many trainees were at the compound, almost to a man.

His total reached thirty-three.

A few were mercs and easy to spot in casual jungle wear, gristled looking, tough and at ease in what might seem to others to be a hostile environment.

The Executioner was more than a little interested in what these men were being trained for.

BOLAN HAD BEEN toting a lot of heavy gear through the Guatemalan jungle for the past few hours. Now the extra effort was going to pay off, because he had arrived at the scene prepared to take on a small army.

One of the most important pieces in his arsenal—and the item that had weighed down his pack the most during the trek from his landing site—was the single-shot McMillan rifle, which fired a .50-caliber, 700-grain round. Bolan quickly assembled the weapon on a slight rise that allowed him to see over most of the buildings. It was the best the relatively flat terrain had to offer in terms of a good firing position. The scope brought the targets up close and very personal.

The soldier was in no hurry, and he spent several long minutes using the scope to scan the compound, getting a feel for the layout, matching the DEA map in his head, sketched from orbital photographs, with the actual buildings on the ground. There were the barracks and the house that served as living quarters for the officers. Three smaller buildings probably served as storage and as quarters for locals who were kept on hand for maintenance, and nearby was the fuel dump and the camouflaged Forger.

It all had to go.

The first order of business was the Forger, but getting at it would be a challenge. The only guards in the compound, besides those in the towers, were a handful of men stationed around the parked aircraft.

What was required was a first-rate distraction, one that would draw everyone's attention from the Forger.

Bolan left the M-88 and spent another half hour moving in a wide quarter-circle around the compound. Once he got near the fuel dump the vegetation thinned and the ground became risky. He had to approach with extreme caution, crawling on his belly from bush to bush. His attention was constantly on the man in the west-end guard tower. Although the gunner didn't seem to have an eye on the dump, any stray glance in Bolan's direction might detect a shaking bush or a shadowy, man form laying among the leaves.

His movement became easier once he reached the dump. There were approximately one hundred fifty-five-gallon barrels parked in neat rows, and at the south end of the barrels was a large aboveground drum on concrete pedestals. That was the fuel for the Forger, he guessed. The drums were probably fuel for the helicopters that landed on the now-empty helipad, between the west tower and the Forger. Sneaking among the rows of fuel, Bolan planted his two radio-controlled detonators and blocks of plastique. One went on the concrete pedestal for the large drum, where the blast would be sure to damage both the big drum and several nearby fifty-five-gallon barrels. The other went among the barrels at the opposite end of the dump. A few light taps assured Bolan that the barrels were still full of fuel. He hoped that the dual explosions would obliterate the dump. That would slow operations significantly, even if he accomplished nothing else during his probe.

Again on his belly, he made his way carefully back into the heavier jungle vegetation, where he could move with comparative ease, although his eyes were peeled for proximity sensors and motion detectors.

By the time the recruits in the compound had finished morning calisthenics and were emerging from breakfast mess, Bolan was back behind the scope of the M-88.

He placed the radio-control mechanism on the ground next to the M-88 and activated it. The tiny red LED glowed in warning. Bolan sighted on the west-end guard tower and retrieved the radio control, depressing the button without looking at the unit.

He heard the twin blasts of the plastique rip through the early morning and watched the tower guard run to the side of the watch platform. With the sound of the explosion still echoing across the compound he fired the M-88. The massive .50-caliber round ejected from the muzzle at a velocity of three thousand feet per second and had an effective range of about three thousand yards. The round dropped more or less as Bolan had estimated and crashed into the guard's torso, punching him onto the guard platform.

With quick, deft movements the Executioner reloaded the M-88 and redirected his aim at the east tower, where the guard was also watching the explosion, an M-16 or similar autorifle in his hands. The tower was slightly farther away, and the shot was somewhat trickier due to the westerly breeze that would affect the travel. He compensated with a sniper's instinct and triggered the massive gun again.

The guard took the round in the chest and staggered across the platform. He hit one of the roof supports in the corner, then fell out of sight.

Bolan jumped to his feet, with what he knew were just moments to spare. The death of the tower guards would be noticed soon enough, and the Forger guards wouldn't spend a long time investigating the explosion of the fuel dump before returning to their posts. Bolan raced down the hill, fully exposed to anyone in the compound who might look in his direction, and sprinted toward the Forger.

The guards were indeed gone, and the soldier glimpsed the conflagration he had caused—fuel smoke crowning the great tongues of yellow and orange flame that rose as tall as the nearby jungle. The men were running around its perimeter, trying to figure out what to do. There was a muffled burst as another barrel blew.

The Executioner approached the edge of the compound, stopping at the point where the vegetation was cleared. He grabbed at the three grenades in his big shirt pocket and heaved them under the camouflaged netting of the parked Russian aircraft, one after another, then retreated as the counts on the grenades ran down. He dived at the one-second mark and landed heavily on all fours as the count for the first fragmentation grenade reached zero. It detonated with an explosion that rocked the compound.

Bolan was still on the move, crawling to better cover before the crowds were attracted to his second act in that morning's play. The second fragger blew, followed almost instantly by the high-explosive grenade. Bolan's hope had been that the first two frags would rip open the fuel cells on the aircraft and that the HE would ignite it.

He crawled to a stop in a low, leafy clump of vegetation, dense enough to hide him, and surveyed his work. The aircraft was burning vigorously along with the camouflage netting, and Bolan knew that the Forger was out of commission for the long-term.

One less major piece of hardware. The odds had been shifted ever so slightly away from the Russians, but not far enough.

Bolan's work was just getting started.

8

Brian Fagen stormed out of his private quarters in camou trousers and combat boots, dragging on a white T-shirt. Gary Albrecht exited the mess tent on the run, staring at the plumes of black smoke in disbelief.

"What's going on?" Fagen demanded.

"I don't know."

Another explosion—this time it did not seem to come from the fuel dump.

"Is that the Forger?" Fagen demanded.

"I don't know."

"Well, go find out!"

There were several subsequent explosions, all of them coming from the direction of the Russian aircraft.

Albrecht was already running in the direction of the explosions. Fagen ducked back inside long enough to grab a shirt and his handgun holster, which he slung over his arm as he made his way quickly toward the Forger.

The VTOL jet was in flames. Tattered holes lined the fuselage and left wing, and a huge section of one of the left-wing thrusters was dangling at an awkward angle. It looked as if some disease had eaten away at it. A sudden hushing sound emanated from the craft, and the many small tongues of flame transformed into a massive fuel fire. The fire was mostly clear, but where it burned the metal and other parts, or mixed with leaking hydraulic fluid, it turned smoky colors. One of the nearby guards, who stood helplessly watching the aircraft burn, screamed as a tongue of flame licked at him. He became an orange specter that seemed to float across the ground, issuing a great, unearthly wail, before collapsing in the thin grass.

Fagen slowed and came to a stop. The Forger was a total loss.

The Russians were going to be angry.

Albrecht yelled at some of the men, and his face was visibly red even from a distance. He pushed one of guards to the ground and kicked him in the ribs. Fagen approached.

"How about you?" Albrecht shouted to one of the guards. "You got an answer?"

"No, boss. I swear to you we didn't do anything. We heard the explosion at the fuel dump, and we thought there was something wrong. When we got there we heard this other explosion. That's all."

"If you would have stayed, you might have been able to keep the fire from reaching the jet, you idiot!"

"It wasn't the dump fire that started the Forger," Fagen said.

Albrecht looked at him, his fury replaced by confusion.

"Grenades were used—those three last explosions we heard."

"Grenades?"

"I'm surprised you didn't recognize the sound, Gary. The fuel fire was a distraction. Somebody set it off knowing that as soon as they did, all the guards around the plane would go running off like a bunch of disobedient children who can't do as they are told. As soon as everybody was gone, he threw in three grenades."

Albrecht was shocked. "Fuck me."

He stomped off in the direction of the west guard tower, shouting up to the guard. He cupped his hand and shouted again. He got no response and looked back at Fagen, communicating exasperation, then started to climb the ladder.

Fagen didn't bother to watch. He knew what his longtime friend would find. He glanced at the other guard tower and saw that there was no guard up there, either.

"Go get the body out of the tower," he said, indicating two of his men. "I want both of you to stay up there. You two, you help Albrecht get this body out and then stand guard there. We've got enemies in the area. Very skilled. Probably keeping low. But they may have left some evidence of themselves out in the open. And I suggest you do a better job this time than you did in your last assignment."

The men hurried off to the towers. The Forger continued to burn, and Fagen knew it might keep going for hours.

He met Albrecht at the base of the guard tower.

"What's your take?" Albrecht asked.

"Antiterrorist squad. Maybe Cuban. Whoever they are, they're skilled and well-armed. They used a long-range sniper's weapon to take out the tower guards, and some heavy-duty explosives. I say they place one guy with a long-range gun, one near the fuel, and another near the jet. The first guy grenades the fuel, the sniper takes out the tower guys during the explosion so we never hear the shots, and the guy at the jet steps out into the open after all the guards have run off. Simple and effective."

"Three guys, you think?" Albrecht asked.

"You think different?"

"I don't know."

Fagen knelt at the corpse of the dead tower guard and withdrew a large fighting knife. He cut the shirt off and examined the entry point of the bullet. It had struck him in the chest on the side of the right pectoral and crashed through the rib cage and heart before coming to a halt.

"The fuel blows," Albrecht suggested, "the guard stepped to the west side of the tower platform to see what's happened, and the sniper fires from…"

They both followed the path of travel, and their eyes landed on the hillock outside the south perimeter of the camp.

"I'm on it," Albrecht said.

"Take five men. Send five more west. Have them fan out for about two, three miles, and meet you southwest of the compound."

"Yes, sir," Albrecht said.

"Listen, Gary, when you get them, figure out who they are, then shoot them dead. Got it?"

"Yeah."

BOLAN WATCHED the two teams move out from the compound and kept a careful watch on the extra tower guards as he made his way down from his hilltop perch. He custom-made a trail for the men who would be following him—a trail that looked like it was made by a skilled hunter, a trail that could only be read by a skilled hunter. Then, when the trail was made, he left it, merging into the grass, leaving no evidence of his passing.

Quickly he wove tall grasses and dried weeds into camouflage headgear, then planted his weapons around him in a copse of tall grass and sank out of sight.

Albrecht and his team arrived minutes later, fanning out from the end of the trail, unable to determine precisely where their prey had disappeared to. One man came within paces of the Executioner's hiding place. So close, Bolan could have reached out and strangled him.

But he stayed deep in the vegetation, making himself so much a part of the jungle that even the insects hovering over him noticed nothing out of the ordinary.

Then Albrecht's men had walked by. Their enemy, their prey, was behind them. The prey became the hunter.

BOLAN HAD COUNTED ten men leaving the compound. Five had started south, in the direction of hill. Somebody sharp had figured out his former sniping position. The other group headed west, in the direction the attacker might have retreated after bombing the fuel dump. They were under the impression that several enemies inhabited the Guatemalan jungles at this moment. Bolan wasn't about to spoil the illusion.

He shrugged off the camouflage covering of dried vegetation and moved through the forest in silence, leaving behind his firearms, except the Beretta 93-R. But he would avoid using even that if at all possible. He was vastly outnumbered, and his advantage lay in serpentlike stealth.

The name of this game was silent attrition, and Bolan had played it before and invariably emerged victorious.

He ignored the trail the group left of broken branches, crushed grasses, prints in the ground and debris on the undergrowth. He found his own way, on hard earth where his feet left no mark and under brush that wasn't disturbed by his passing. He was quite possibly wasting his time. The group had already passed, and there was no reason to think that others might come in pursuit of him along this way, but there were times his warrior's instinct told him it couldn't hurt to be too cautious.

Soon he was within sight of the first victim, the last man of the five, on the far left flank of the group and a good hundred feet from the nearest searcher. He was a brutal-looking giant of a man, dark-complected and black-haired, with a face so scarred and distorted it looked like a mask. He hadn't lived an easy life, carrying the experience of countless battles in his stance, in the shifting of his eyes, in the very aura surrounding him.

Bolan observed the man from a distance and from the cover of the low growth, assessing his opponent's alertness and canniness. It was tough to call from simply watching the man march through the jungle, but easy to see when the scar-faced man stopped to look at the leaves on a weed that would have said nothing to an untrained tracker; when he pulled aside ground grasses to look at a patch of bare earth for tracks that an unskilled man would never have thought to look for.

The soldier crept across the ground, moving from brush to brush with one fist invariably hovering near the fighting knife sheathed on his hip.

He moved to within thirty paces of the scar-faced hunter and stopped at the trunk of a large tree, where he scanned through the jungle for the next searcher. They were well-trained and instructed. The distance between them was consistent so far—within earshot of a shout.

But not close enough to hear a dying gasp. Bolan intended to allow Scarface no more than that.

Scarface had halted in a clearing. He squatted and as Bolan moved in closer, he watched the man running the palm of his hands over the short, fine grasses that covered the soft earth of the clearing. He was looking for indentations so slight they could not even be seen, only felt.

But of course he wouldn't find them. The distance was at twenty paces. Bolan waited. The man seemed to be staring at the open space. Or, perhaps, he was listening. The Executioner was sure he had approached in silence, but even the most skilled jungle warrior could fail to avoid a hunter's instinct.

Scarface stood and twisted to scan the jungle behind him. Bolan moved fully behind the tree trunk and listened. There was no sound. Scarface was either extraordinarily silent when he moved, or he was still standing at the edge of the tiny clearing.

Bolan guessed it was the latter, and he waited as well. Often, impatience was the catalyst to deadly mistakes. Bolan wasn't one to make mistakes, and while patience wasn't a natural attribute of his personality, he had learned it as a skill. He stood in the jungle with the morning getting warmer, listening to the voices of the birds and other wildlife.

The wait lasted seven minutes.

The subtle game continued. Scarface finally moved on, and Bolan waited for him to take a half-dozen steps before continuing after him—and now he would see how skilled the man truly was. Because Scarface would feel the need to catch up to the rest of his group. He couldn't move fast quietly....

His footsteps became rushed, stomping through the underbrush quickly, scanning side to side in a comparably cursory manner. He might easily have missed the signs of a skilled man's passing, and he entirely missed the sound of skilled man coming behind him.

Bolan approached to within ten paces as the weeds thrashed at Scarface's ankles.

There was a shout up ahead and to the right. Scarface shouted back, "Yeah?"

"Where are you?"

Bolan moved faster under the cover of the loud voices, watching his prey's back but watching the ground more closely for weeds and brush that would sound his approach.

"I'm coming."

"You find something?"

Bolan twisted sideways to pass between two tiny tree branches without making them so much as quiver, then straightened again at only two paces from Scarface.

"No, I didn't find anything."

The Ka-bar blade came out of its sheath, the blade flat black, as if it were a piece of shadow or an object upon which the sun refused to shine.

"Well, get with the group!"

The blade hung in the air at shoulder level and Bolan took another step closer.

"I'm comin'!"

The Ka-bar swept downward, and at the very last second Scarface had to have heard the passage of the weapon through the atmosphere. He started to jerk in its direction, but he was too late. The blade slammed into its target, penetrating the neck musculature and windpipe. Bolan jerked the blade, and Scarface collapsed into him. The soldier bore the body to the ground, pulling the blade deeply through the flesh to hasten the kill.

One down.

Nine to go.

AL WHITE WAS WATCHING the path, but he was looking for snakes more closely than he was watching for signs of the gang that had bombed the compound.

He had felt pretty tough when he got back from Desert Storm, a decorated Marine, and when Albrecht recruited him for the mercenary group based in Central America, White had swallowed the romanticism of it all, hook, line and sinker.

What could be cooler than being a professional soldier, outside the law, living the hard life with gusto? His moral qualms were few and far between—one of the primary attributes Albrecht had been looking for. White could kill anybody that needed to be killed if it was part of the job. He'd leave the decision-making and moralizing to others.

It was the jungle that got to him. He'd never had to deal with it when he was in the Middle East. It was all desert— hot and dry and few creatures crawling around in it. The jungle…well, he never would have admitted that it frightened him.

The truth was, he was scared to death of snakes, spiders, all the massive biting bugs that roamed the swampy woods. He couldn't stand any of it. He was going to get out of here as soon as his contract with Albrecht expired. That couldn't come fast enough.

He heard the sounds of footsteps off to his left. What the hell was Villichez up to? First he was dragging behind, and now he was getting way too close.

"What're you doing now?" he called, although he didn't take his eyes from his path. There was no answer.

Villichez wasn't just moving in too close, he was coming to join White. Maybe he'd found something.

"What're you doing, man?" he asked.

Villichez didn't answer, and White finally stopped to see what, exactly, the man was doing.

It wasn't Villichez at all. It was a big guy with blue eyes and dark hair, and for a half second White thought he was one of Albrecht's newer guys.

The dark-haired man stepped within arm's reach and suddenly a huge, bloodstained, anodized knife came into view. White gasped, about to scream, but then the knife slammed into his gut and ripped up into his lungs and the air left his body in a rush. He fell into the weeds and the mud, and his last thought was that he was going to lie in the jungle forever with the snakes and the spiders and the worms consuming him.

BOLAN'S TIME WAS SHORT. His first two victims had carried walkie-talkies, and he knew it wouldn't be long before someone would be expecting them to check in. He didn't want the alarm raised prematurely. He moved through the jungle like a panther, silent and swift, passing well behind the group leader and moving to the man marching on his right flank. Bolan planted himself in the shadows of a tree trunk directly in the man's path and let him march into his ambush. He wasn't putting much effort into the search, barely scanning from side to side. He never saw death coming for him until it was too late.

The Executioner emerged from behind the tree trunk as the man walked past, grabbing him by the chin and pulling his head up, drawing the skin of the throat taut. The knife blade slid through the flesh easily. The man went to the ground without a struggle, as if he had been ready for death all along and was more than willing to accept it.

His walkie-talkie buzzed seconds after he died. Bolan took it and moved ahead in the jungle, intent on finding the source.

ALBRECHT LISTENED and tried again.

There was no reply. He stopped in the jungle and looked behind him, although none of his men should have been within visual range.

"White? Villichez? Come in."

Nothing.

"Somebody give me a reply, now," he said, exasperated.

No reply was given.

Albrecht considered the situation briefly. He wasn't going to call back to the camp, and he wasn't going to call for help from the other squad. He was second in command, and he wouldn't allow himself to look helpless. There had to be a reasonable explanation for the silence, and he would figure it out before he went crying for backup.

He hooked the walkie-talkie on his belt and held the M-16 with two hands, ready to fire, as he backtracked through the woods. Franke ought to be somewhere in that direction.

The woods were quiet and peaceful, and Albrecht stifled his temptation to yell, not wanting to give himself away. Besides, this would provide him the chance to sneak up on Franke, see how aware the kid really was. He was desert-experienced, like his buddy White, and Albrecht didn't trust his jungle presence.

He reached a point in the woods where Franke would appear if he were still on his correct heading. He leaned against a soft, fallen log, casually, only partially hidden by a bush, and he made no move for a full two minutes.

FRANKE SILENCED the walkie-talkie with a swift movement of his hand and stood stock-still in the jungle, his eyes peeled. He'd explain to Albrecht later. Right now he was sure he was being tracked.

He wasn't sure yet what had warned him of the presence of the predator—maybe a slight change in the ambient jungle sounds, maybe the sound of a predator's breath too quiet to be identified by his conscious mind but loud enough to set off instinctive alarms. Whatever it was, the instinct was strong. His heart was pounding and his breathing growing faster despite his best efforts to stay silent, and he moved into the bushes and waited for a minute for the predator to show itself. There was no sound or movement during that entire minute.

Franke stepped out of the bushes.

He resumed his pace through the jungle, more alert than ever. But it seemed that the jungle had lost its restlessness. The predator, perhaps, had moved on.

He took out the walkie-talkie and turned it on. There was no sound from it, and as he raised it to his face, his vision sped to the left, were there had been some sort of movement he couldn't define. He turned off the walkie-talkie again and put it away.

The movement didn't repeat itself. Maybe it had been a breeze shaking a branch.

Franke heard something ahead of him about fifty or sixty feet, and, in a crouchwalk, pursued it.

TWO MEN WERE LEFT.

One was sitting in the brush twenty feet away, waiting, Bolan assumed, for the appearance of one of his companions, who had yet to appear. Neither of them knew that they were the only two survivors.

The second five-man team was somewhere to the north across the jungle. Bolan intended to go after them next. Then, when the time came to infiltrate the compound itself, he could be sure that reinforcement wasn't imminent. He could strike with impunity.

The American in the bushes pulled a cigar out of his shirt pocket and clamped down on it, allowing his eyes to wander through the landscape of flora momentarily. He removed the cigar, spit out a piece of tobacco and replaced it in his teeth.

Bolan had hoped to wait until the two men were together, then he could take them out quickly and cleanly. There was no one around to hear him use the 93-R.

But he wasn't going to wait any longer. He had a lot to get done and not all that much time to do it. He crept through the underbrush with the Beretta up and ready.

As the man in the bushes scanned the jungle for his companion, Bolan moved to within five feet.

The man in the bushes suddenly whirled on him, leveling the M-16, and Bolan stepped lightly to the right, putting a mass of growth between them. The M-16 fired briefly, but the man was unable to force good aim through the brush, and Bolan was already leveling the 93-R. He triggered once low and rode out the recoil of the triburst, which carried the aim progressively higher, and all three rounds crashed through the thick growth of the bush and into Gary Albrecht. He fell through the branches, landing on his back in the open.

FRANKE FROZE at the sound of gunfire and the heavy thud of a body hitting the ground. A glance out of his own cover showed him Gary Albrecht landing on his back with at least three bloody holes down his front, his M-16 tumbling out of his hands. Albrecht was staring into the jungle canopy with stone-still eyes.

Franke made a quick assessment of the source of the fire that had killed Albrecht and aimed his Uzi. Four bursts ripped through the jungle and emptied the mag.

BOLAN DROPPED into the dirt and let the round drill the air above him—all of them were directed at a far-off point anyway. Then he heard the sound of a single soldier crashing away through the jungle.

9

The Guatemalan mercenary knelt by the body and peered at the open space under the neck, assuring himself there were no wires there before passing the length of rope under it. He wrapped the rope around Albrecht's neck, just tightly enough that it wouldn't slip over his chin, and tied it. Then he walked back to the others, trailing the rope behind him.

Franke was jerking his head back and forth, looking for the killers he knew inhabited the jungle. He didn't feel much safer having the five men from the second team with him. He didn't see what benefit could be gained by returning to base with Albrecht's body. Why risk moving it at all if it might be booby-trapped?

"Ready?" asked the American leader of the group.

"*Sí*, yes," the man with the rope replied. Franke backed away from the group as they stepped behind the protective cover of trees, and the man with the rope tightened the slack. He carefully pulled on it. Albrecht's neck stretched grotesquely, then his entire body, and he slithered across the ground. Another man got on the rope and Albrecht was speeding across the open toward them.

There was no depression where his body had lain—a depression that might have been filled with explosives. The group gathered around the corpse with the makeshift litter they had improvised from branches and rope.

They knew Fagen wouldn't give a damn about the other corpses, but he would want the body of his old friend brought to him. If they didn't bring it now, they would just be sent back for it when they returned to the compound. They were saving themselves some trouble.

Bolan watched from thirty yards. The American he had scared away the first time was keeping his distance, but all the others were as near as they were going to get. He couldn't wait any longer and risk his surprise being discovered and deactivated. He actuated the radio control in his pocket.

THE BODY of Gary Albrecht was about to be rolled onto the framework of branches when it exploded. The two men bending over him received the brunt of the blast and were flung backward, landing dead on their backs. The three remaining men ran away from the blast, two of them screaming. Bolan ignored the screamers. They had been blinded, at least temporarily. He moved across the jungle in a trot after the quiet one, the man who had escaped relatively unharmed.

The man ducked behind a tree and came to a halt, breathing hard, then looked around the trunk again, back the way he had come. There was a red streak across his shoulders.

Bolan aimed through the brush and fired. The first single round from the 93-R slammed into the trunk of the tree inches from the gunman's face and sent him reeling back. He stumbled over weeds and windmilled his free arm wildly for balance. Bolan tracked him and fired again, the round this time crashing into his rib cage, high up, ripping at the pectoral muscle. The man fell into a sitting position in the weeds and triggered his Uzi blindly into the jungle in two short bursts.

Bolan dodged to his right to avoid the fire pattern and lost the man momentarily in the growth. Then he stepped into the open and achieved acquisition on the sitting target at the moment the gunner spotted him. The 93-R triggered before the Uzi, and the gunman fell on his back. Bolan ran toward the fallen man and fired again when he spotted the Uzi being raised. The arm dropped. The soldier stood over the gunman and saw that he was dead, glassy eyes staring up at him devoid of life.

He moved back in the direction of the explosion, where he

found one of the blinded men on his belly, his lifeblood seeping into the earth.

There was a loud scream, and Bolan went in search of the noise, quickly coming upon the other blind man, who was bouncing from tree to tree, snatching at leaves and branches and using his arm to try to clear the blood from his vision. The victim's eyes were essentially burned out, and the face was blackened by the plastique blast.

Amazingly he wasn't entirely blind. He came to a sudden halt as Bolan stepped out of the trees and faced him down from a distance of twenty feet. He shook his head and squinted through the jungle with one fragmented corner of an eyeball that still seemed to retain function. He stopped whimpering and wiped his face savagely, then squinted at Bolan again.

Suddenly he grabbed at the holster under his left arm and dragged out a 9 mm combat pistol.

Bolan stepped to the side and approached the man from an angle as he squinted into the jungle, trying to locate his enemy again.

"Where are you? Show yourself, you son of a bitch!" he shouted.

"Right here," Bolan said from just paces away. The man whirled at the spot and fired the 9 mm wildly, sending the Executioner into a crouch. He fired up at the blind man, who collapsed and lay motionless.

Bolan inspected the site of the explosion. The mercenaries had been experienced enough to consider the possibility of a booby-trapped body, but not wary enough to realize their adversary would have used a variance on the old jungle warfare trick—radio-controlled remote explosives that weren't common military issue during the jungle wars.

The two men who had been closest to the blast had never even felt the explosion. Not much was left of them, nor of Albrecht's corpse.

The only one who had survived the onslaught was the American gunman, who had been too afraid to stay with the group.

Bolan knew the man was hightailing it back to the base camp, which was the warrior's next stop, as well.

BRIAN FAGEN HOISTED Franke to his feet by the collar and backhanded him. The man spun 180 degrees and collapsed, heaving. He pushed himself to his hands and knees and vomited in the dusty soil. Fagen kicked him onto his back.

"Where are the others?" he demanded again.

Franke was gasping for air. He had stormed into the camp just a minute before, exhausted and hyperventilating, weaponless and scarred with scrapes and cuts that came from running blindly through the jungle for miles. "Dead!" he gasped.

"What about the other team?"

Franke closed his eyes and shook his head violently. "All dead. Both teams are dead!"

"What about Albrecht?"

Franke opened his eyes. "Blew him up. He rigged his body with explosives and blew him to pieces."

Fagen stared at the prostrate man, but he didn't seem to see him anymore.

"He's one bad son of a bitch," Franke said.

"One?" Fagen snapped to awareness. "Why do you think it's just one man?"

"That's all I saw was one man. When the body blew up I saw just one guy. A big, dark-haired guy. He executed the others, the ones who survived the blast. There was nobody else."

"You trying to tell me one guy wiped out nine men in the course of a few hours?"

Franke didn't try to push the point. He lay in the dirt gasping for breath.

Fagen shook his head, then laughed bitterly. It sounded like a bark.

He turned to the other men—sixteen seasoned mercenaries, four more in the watchtowers, plus the trainees.

A jungle fight was one thing. If the one-man execution

squad tried getting into these grounds, with this army waiting for him, he'd see what real fighting was all about.

THE LIGHTING SYSTEM made the compound as bright as day in the jungle night. But the west tower was near the jungle's edge, and the lighting system illuminated only a four-yard stretch of ground between the base of the tower and the foliage.

It was a flaw Bolan planned on exploiting.

The probe was fraught with risk, but it was the best available strategy. He would make the best of it and hope it played out long enough for him to inflict some serious damage.

Serious damage was all he could hope for. There was little chance he would be able to wipe out the entire compound. But if he shattered it and made it useless, he would have removed one of the strongest arms of the body that was scheduled to attack the Cuban government.

He didn't know what the mercenaries' target was. Maybe this was the squad that intended to infiltrate Havana's top-level government offices. They were skilled enough that, with inside information and KGB-supplied hardware, success wasn't out of the question.

From a comfortable crook in the low branch of a jungle tree that ascended at least another hundred feet above him, Bolan watched the globe of the sun turn orange, then red, and sink into the distant horizon of the jungle.

He began to refresh the combat cosmetics that would render him virtually invisible in the night.

Dusk became darkness, and the various predators of the jungle went on the prowl.

BOLAN CREPT through the brush quietly coming to the edge, within easy reach of the west watchtower. He planted himself there with all his gear and took out the infrared night-vision binoculars, making a quick survey of the watchtower guards.

Two men were in each tower. They looked bored but somewhat attentive, and Bolan knew he had to pick his moment carefully.

It came soon enough. The men in the tower above him disappeared from his low-angled point of view. A quick check told him the guards in the east tower were looking in the other direction. A scan of the compound showed no other guards or mercs in evidence.

He grabbed his pack and moved through the four yards of well-lit open ground in a heartbeat, then tossed the pack over his shoulder and began the strenuous work of quickly and silently climbing the tower.

Within seconds he had climbed above the area lit by the nearby floods and into darkness. He paused on the ladder to listen for sounds of alert.

There was none. So far, the probe was clandestine.

The ladder went up the side wall of the watchtower, and Bolan stopped just beneath it to secure his pack. He withdrew the 93-R. The suppressed weapon was still loud enough for the sound to reach others in the compound. Being who they were, they just might recognize the strange retort for what it was. On the other hand he couldn't allow any warning or cry to come from the tower guards before he took them out.

He raised himself above the side of the wall, bringing the 93-R up beside him and evaluating the guards. One looked away; the other was staring directly at him. The Executioner triggered the 93-R and the first man took the 9 mm round in the chest, falling on his face. The second man was just turning when a round drilled into him, slamming him to the planks of the platform. Bolan launched himself over the wall and checked the guards for vital signs. Both men were dead.

The tower was taken and, as far as Bolan could tell, the camp was unaware of his presence.

Time for the probe to begin in earnest.

He made quick work of positioning the corpses against the wall and posts so that they gave the illusion of life if one didn't watch them for more than a few seconds. Then he went over the side and down the ladder, watching the west tower through the binoculars for his moment. When he was sure both guards were facing away he descended into the light, hit the ground and strode to the north. He was soon behind the large, well-lit houses that served as the quarters for the mercenary leaders. He had only to keep the buildings between himself and the east tower and he knew he would remain unseen.

At the corner he stopped to assure himself the grounds were empty, and moved in a large half circle to get from the house to the barracks without moving into the range of vision of the east tower. He flattened against the building and assessed his plan of attack.

His options were limited.

The rear door of the barracks opened and a sleepy-looking man emerged, heading for the outhouse ten yards away. He didn't see Bolan until he reached it, opened the door and stepped inside. Bolan had the 93-R trained on him and waited for the instant he spotted recognition in the man's face, then he triggered twice in rapid succession and the two suppressed rounds crashed into his chest and pelvis, shaking him like a boneless creature and pushing him into the outhouse. The door spring whined and slammed shut with a crack of flimsy wood.

A cry sounded inside the barracks and Bolan knew his luck had turned. He holstered the 93-R and brought the M-16 into firing position while rummaging in his pack for hand grenades. He pulled the first pin and lobbed the grenade at the nearest open window, where it tore through a ragged screen and landed inside with a metallic sound, immediately followed by a shout of alarm.

Bolan ran the length of the long, low building. He flung another grenade at the fourth window, and in that moment there was a burst of fire and flame from behind him. The barracks was transformed into a dungeon of howling horror as the phosphorous grains flew into the men and began burning through them with unquenchable fire. It ate like acid through tissue and bone. The second grenade blew and the screams magnified, while plumes of smoke and fire began pouring from the windows and the open door. The Executioner tossed a final grenade through the last window, then ran around the end of the building. He spotted a single man fleeing into the open from the barracks and triggered the assault rifle, the rounds chopping into the runner's feet and legs and sending him sprawling in the dirt as the third phosphorous grenade exploded.

The building was brick, but the roof was thatched and within seconds the entire structure was ablaze. Men were pouring chaotically from the inferno, screaming and clawing at themselves, but Bolan couldn't concern himself with them now. With the phosphorous eating at their bodies they were helpless.

His attention went to the east tower, where the guards were peering down at the chaos, easily spotting Bolan if for no other reason than he was the only calm man in sight. He triggered the M-16 briefly in their direction as two quick paces took him behind a small storage building, which was blackened but still standing after the morning fuel dump fire. He found more grenades of a different type in his pockets. These 40 mm high explosive grenades were designed to fit into the M-203 grenade launcher mounted conveniently under the muzzle of the M-16. Bolan fed one of the HEs into the breech and stepped into the open long enough to aim for the east tower and trigger. The round was almost perfectly aimed, and it detonated among the tall wooden tower supports.

BRIAN FAGEN RAN out the front door of his house and around the corner with his handgun drawn. The barracks roof was blazing end to end, and screams of agony came from within, while a half-dozen men were on the ground outside moaning and thrashing—or dead. The attacker had phosphorous grenades!

A rattle of gunfire from the west tower drew the merc leader's attention. The guards were firing at the ground near the shed on the far side of the burning barracks. Fagen started when the gunfire was interrupted by a blast. The tower was suddenly a legless monster that tipped inward and collapsed, the guards screaming. It hit the ground with a tremendous crash of splintering wood. Fagen dodged to the left to avoid the flying debris and leaped over the body of one of the screaming, dying barracks victims and raced around the barracks' end.

BOLAN SPOTTED the newcomer—sandy-haired, early-fifties—and swung the M-16 A-1/M-203 in his direction, emptying the mag at his feet and failing to make contact. The merc had seen it coming and pulled back in time to save himself. Bolan grabbed a fresh mag and clicked it into place, then fed another HE round into the grenade launcher. He targeted the open ground around the corner of the burning barracks and triggered, hoping to land the grenade just in front of the newcomer and catch him in the blast. The HE detonated, and Bolan followed it at once, only to catch the heels-flying retreat of the newcomer, who for a second time in five seconds avoided death by virtue of his lightning-fast reflexes. The fleeing man swung behind the far end of the barracks and was out of sight.

Across the compound two parked four-wheel-drive vehicles came to life and turned on their lights, jumping out of their parking places. Bolan fed a buckshot round into the M-203 and faced down the 4WD that barreled directly at him. With a burst of fire from the M-16 A-1 he forced the driver to steer to the side, and the quick swerve brought the doorless driver's side of the vehicle into view. Bolan triggered the buckshot round and blasted the driver dead instantly, as well as shredding the tires. The 4WD collapsed on two rims and flipped on its side.

The other vehicle was heading across the compound, away from Bolan. The soldier fed another HE round into the M-203 but didn't have time to use it before the 4WD was gone behind one of the buildings. He sprinted in pursuit and spotted a gunman emerging, triggering an AK-74. Bolan fired the M-16 and cut across the gunner's stomach before he could make the AK fire count.

The 4WD careened into view again, this time with a familiar

face in the back seat—it was the sandy-haired man who had dodged his fire just minutes ago. The face matched the computer image Stony Man had provided of Brian Fagen.

The leader of the mercs was making an escape.

Bolan ran after the 4WD, and Fagen raised a large handgun. The Executioner heeled to a stop, aiming and firing the M-203 in what appeared to be a single fluid movement. Fagen saw the action and shouted at the driver, who swerved wildly and managed to steer out of the way of what would have been a dead hit. The HE round detonated feet from the 4WD, and the rear passengers ducked out of sight as their rear window imploded. Somehow the tires escaped terminal damage, and the 4WD accelerated down the dirt road that disappeared into the jungle.

The breeze had carried the burning thatch from the barracks to the two small houses, which were now beginning to blaze themselves. The shed Bolan had used for protection and the splintered rubble of the east tower were also beginning to burn.

He stood alone in the conflagration, watched over only by two men in the west tower.

But their eyes were staring out into the distance, beyond the conflagration of the warrior's making, beyond the jungle, beyond the night.

10

It wasn't long past midnight and the city of Orange Walk, Belize, was growing sleepy.

The dual iron gates swung open under a remote-control signal and a single four-wheel-drive vehicle crowded through them, nearly scraping the paint on either side, coming to a quick halt with a squeal of brakes. Brian Fagen stepped out of the passenger side and slammed the door behind him, surprising the young man who had come to greet him. Fagen raised a hand for silence and stomped inside the city town house before the iron gates to the courtyard had even begun to swing shut.

"What's going on?" Sancho asked of one of the other men exiting the 4WD.

"The Carapito base was attacked," one of Fagen's personal bodyguards, a huge Venezuelan, answered quietly.

"Attacked?"

"Yeah."

"Explain! What do you mean, attacked?"

"What does it sound like? Somebody came in—very skilled, lots of explosives. He blew up the place, starting with the fuel dump this morning. We sent a bunch of guys into the jungle to track him down and only one of them came back. Then after dark the whole place started going up. He blew the barracks with everybody inside. Blew the towers. Blew the whole fucking place."

Sancho was dumb with disbelief, running his fingers through his very dark, long hair.

"The Forger?" he asked finally.

"The Forger went this morning with the fuel dump."

"Oh, shit."

"Yeah."

"How many survivors?"

"How many you count?" the Venezuelan asked.

Sancho looked at the four men who were standing around the courtyard uneasily, unsure what to do with themselves, and then he understood.

"You shitting me, man?"

"I'm not shitting you. He got everybody else. Most of them he got in the barracks, like I said. They were all in there, and he blew them all at once."

"He?"

"Yeah."

"There was just one man."

"There was more than just one guy," one of the other bodyguards said fervently. "There had to be more than just one guy to do all that damage. We just didn't see the rest of them. We just saw the one guy with the grenade launcher. Almost tagged us with the damn thing before we cleared out."

Sancho looked at the brick driveway and said aloud, but to himself, "The Russian trainees are dead, then, too. Five trainees and the aircraft. That's some heavy losses. The Russians aren't going to be too pleased to hear it."

"MY PARTNERS AREN'T going to be too pleased to hear about it," Fagen said.

"No shit, my man. What're you going to do?"

"That's why I'm calling you, Thad. I need your help. I need to call in a few favors."

"Exactly what do you have in mind?"

"I need some men, Thad. I want to fulfill my part of the bargain as best I can. I am *not* going to let myself get scared away from a job."

"Sounds like maybe you ought to be scared away from this job. Sounds like there's some heavy pressure coming down on this operation. Sounds like you got some special forces on your ass. Maybe U.S. Maybe Cuban. Maybe you even got some Russians coming in to try and clean up the mess before it results in bad publicity for them.''

''I don't give a shit. I made a bargain and I intend to stick by it. And I intend to identify and locate today's perpetrator and kick his ass. You owe me a few major favors if I remember correctly.''

''That's right, I do—but I don't like the idea of throwing my men away. What guarantee do I have that they won't end up dead, like your guys at Carapito?''

''Don't worry about that. I won't be going back to Carapito, for one thing.''

''Then where'll you be doing preparation?''

''My partners have a place. I'll inform you in a few hours where to send your men. They'll meet up with the rest of my men in the morning and transport to the new base.''

''Wait, wait a second—how many men we talking here?''

''All you can spare.''

''I got nothing going down now. I can spare a significant number.''

''Send them all,'' Fagen said, ''and then we'll say we're even.''

Thad had to have been thinking it over. ''Yeah. Okay. I'll send them. I'm trusting you not to lose me all my men, Fagen.''

''You're not going to lose all your men, Thad. You can take that to the bank.''

Fagen sat staring at the phone for a long minute after hanging up. Calling in favors from the leader of another mercenary band had been the easy call. It had involved nothing more than a little swallowed pride. The next call would be considerably more difficult.

He dialed, got an international connection and finally got an answer.

''Give me General Resnikoff,'' he said. ''Yeah, it's important. Wake him up.''

BOLAN HAD TO GIVE Brian Fagen credit. He had to have run a reasonably successful operation to be able to afford high-quality equipment. The 4WD he'd appropriated from the compound was an all-out powerhouse with all the upgrades. The leftover vehicles met with destruction with a single carefully planted high explosive grenade.

All Bolan left standing when he exited the Carapito compound, less than fifteen minutes after the hurried flight of the last survivor, was the single watchtower with its ghoulish watchkeeps. The dead watching over the dead.

He appreciated the capabilities of the 4WD increasingly as he left the highway to go off-road across the northern stretch of Guatemalan territory and across the border into Mexico. The bumpy ride didn't slow him substantially and by 1:00 a.m. he was on the highway again, heading northeast. He paused at 1:15 a.m. just long enough to appropriate license plates from a VW parked in front of a small, dark roadside house.

By 2:00 a.m. he had located the Mexican enclave of Brian Fagen's mercenary organization.

It was a smart move stationing his men in various locales in the neighboring nations, but Fagen might have chosen more insular locations. Then again, he had never counted on a one-man execution force targeting him.

Bolan again had the benefit of a DEA-supplied map of the enclave—three small haciendas grouped around a patch of bare, dry dirt. He estimated twelve or fifteen men could be housed on the spot comfortably, but spotted a dry patch of grass where it appeared a tent had stood at one time. With army tents for barracks and mess, the operation population of this facility might be quadrupled.

Now that the Guatemalan locale was compromised, Fagen might attempt to move his men here.

Bolan didn't want that to happen, which was why this spot was on his to-do list. He anticipated a skeletal staff, which would be awake, having been notified of the problems at Carapito. There was even a chance that Fagen had fled here, but Bolan doubted it.

He headed for the enclave at a steady thirty miles per hour and flashed his lights at the guard with an Uzi slung over his left shoulder.

The guard asked for ID in Spanish.

"Fagen sent me."

"Bullshit!" the guard responded, leveling the Uzi with surprisingly quick reflexes. Bolan raised the prepped 93-R from his lap and fired out the window one time. The cough of the suppressed, subsonic round was predominantly contained inside the 4WD, and Bolan knew it wouldn't reach the enclave. The guard fell back into the darkness, heart mangled by the close-range, dead-on shot.

Bolan put the 4WD in neutral and turned off the engine, drifting into the enclave with only the sounds of the tires chewing on gravel, and parking in the moon shadows behind the one dark building.

He holstered the 93-R and grabbed the M-16 A-1/M-203, which was bulkier than he would have preferred for a short-range interior battle. He'd make do.

Several long strides took him to the first of the illuminated buildings. A quick look into an uncurtained window revealed four men. He tried the doorknob, finding it unlocked. He twisted it and kicked open the door.

Three of the men sat in the one-room building, a fourth lounged on one of the rear bunks, and all of them leaped to their feet in the instant it took for the door to swing into the wall with a bang.

Bolan targeted the first gun he saw and triggered the M-16 A-1, which chopped into the gunman twice, flinging him to the floor. His nearer comrade hefted a handgun, and Bolan took him out with a single shot to the heart, then blasted at the third man, catching him in the shoulder as he dived for cover. The wound didn't even slow him, and he got to his feet firing his .38 Smith & Wesson. The M-16 A-1 fired again and the gunman ate the bullet, screaming through the sudden flood of blood pouring from his throat into his mouth and lungs. That round didn't down him either. He staggered and brought his handgun into target acquisition at the same instant the sleeping man finally dragged a snub-nosed Browning out of his pants and aimed it at Bolan.

The Executioner aimed between them and triggered the buckshot round in the M-203. The load of double-aught projectiles reduced the two gunmen to cooling flesh instantly.

"WHAT THE HELL was that?" Crusat shouted.

"I don't know!" Arias answered, making a grab for his handgun.

"What's happening! What's going on!" It was Fagen, voice screaming from the phone receiver in his hand.

"Go find out!" Crusat ordered, then said into the phone, "We're under attack."

"It's the same guy," Fagen said.

"How do you know?"

"It is. I'm patching through to video. Go kill that bastard!"

"Yeah." Crusat dropped the phone and grabbed his Uzi from the shelf and sprinted toward the door as he heard another burst of fire from the adjacent building. He peered out, just in time to witness a man with an M-16 trigger the weapon in full-auto mode. Arias was taking the rounds, rattling on his feet like he was in an earthquake. Then he dropped to the dirt, bleeding in a dozen places. The gunman disappeared.

Crusat heard nothing but ominous silence as he scanned the street. The others were already dead. If the American had killed the men in the adjacent building, who did that leave?

He heard the boxy thrum of Uzi-fire and glimpsed one of the road guards running blindly in the direction of the enclave. He was in the open, firing blindly at the building. Crusat knew the guard hadn't taken his training to heart; he was as good as dead.

The mag in the running guard's Uzi was dry in seconds, and he found himself in the middle of the road, helpless and unarmed. The American realized it as well, and stepped out of the building and triggered the M-16 at the guard as he dived for cover, cutting him dead before he crashed into the dirt.

A gunshot sounded behind Bolan and he twisted, falling back into the doorway just in time to see the door of the adjacent building closing rapidly. He triggered his next buckshot round. Most of the fifty pellets slammed into the wooden door and the earth, but a good number of them disappeared inside the building, eliciting a scream of agony.

He thumbed another buckshot into the breech of the M-203 and pushed at the tattered, swinging door. There was a single survivor in the room, suffering from several pellet wounds to the face and chest. He turned drunkenly at the sound of Bolan's entrance and staggered into a table. He doubled over it, mouth open wide in a silent scream of agony, and painfully positioned his Uzi to fire single-handed in his adversary's general direction.

Bolan took one step in the gunman's direction and triggered the M-203, the round taking Crusat's life like a tiny candle snuffed with a giant hand.

The soldier stood silent for a moment. The enclave was deathly still.

Then he spotted a glimmer of glass across the room, where a video surveillance camera was mounted, a tiny red dot of light glowing.

Bolan aimed the M-16 A-1 and triggered a single round that reduced the camera to scrap parts.

FAGEN WATCHED IN HORROR at the surreal images transmitting from Mexico. Over the phone lines the fuzzy black-and-white digitized video came through at just eight frames per second, giving the action the jumpy appearance of an old silent slapstick film.

But this was no Keystone Kops. The violence was real, immediate and personal.

The outside camera had shown the guard running toward the enclave and then get shot down as he tried to scramble for cover.

Then Fagen switched to the second bungalow. He saw only dead men—and the back of their killer at the doorway.

He switched to the first bungalow and watched Crusat, alone now, retreat through the doorway. Suddenly there was a blast coming through the door. Did he have a shotgun, too?

No, it was a grenade launcher, firing buckshot rounds, mounted under an M-16. Better than a shotgun.

Fagen felt an icy coldness in his gut, then the chill crawled up his spine.

Jerkily he saw Crusat make a desperate move with his sub-gun. Like a silent-movie Frankenstein, the dark figure with the heavy hardware strode in Crusat's direction. He didn't even flinch at the Uzi aiming at him. That was a sign of something.

There was a blast from the grenade launcher, and Fagen felt like throwing up. That bastard had just fired a buckshot round into Crusat from about a yard-and-a-half. That was brutal.

The dark figure stood still for a moment. He wasn't contemplating the lives he had snuffed out. He was listening for others. Apparently he heard nothing.

Then he spotted the camera and, for a moment, Fagen and the dark man were seeing eye to eye.

There could be no more doubt. Fagen recognized him as the same man he had run away from just hours earlier at Carapito.

The dark figure aimed his weapon squarely at the camera and the screen turned to snow.

JUAN ORIOL KNOCKED lightly on the heavy wooden door and stepped into the office. General Javier Serra glanced up and gave him a brief wave, gesturing for him to sit. He chose the comfortably upholstered chair and sat heavily.

"Not that one, please," the general said, gesturing to the highly polished leather chair next to it.

Oriol got up and moved over.

"I could never get the stains out of the material," the general said, adding his signature to the paper in front of him with a flourish.

Oriol didn't understand the reference and his attention was drawn to the fact that there was someone behind him, when he had thought he was alone in the office with the general. As he turned to see who the third party was he felt the distinctive cold touch of a gun barrel jammed into the side of his skull.

He looked at the general with wide eyes. The general tossed him a pair of handcuffs.

"Put them on."

Oriol did so. The general pointed a remote control at the bookcase built into the wall, and a small television set turned on. The image it played was strange at first, then Oriol recognized it as the office he was in right now, but seen at night and from directly overhead. Someone entered the room and began going through the drawers of the desk.

"We weren't even sure who it was at first," the general said. "Then we got lucky. Right...here."

The figure on the screen closed the drawer and looked up, scanning the room. The features were very clear. It was Oriol himself. His entire covert probe caught on videotape.

He rolled his eyes to the ceiling, and his gaze fell on the smoke detector with the small, dark opening in the center.

"You've got it," the general said. "You should have spotted it sooner." He aimed the remote and the television screen went black again.

"Who sent you?" the general demanded.

Oriol said nothing.

"Are you army Intelligence? DGA?"

Oriol looked at the general and was silent.

The general looked at the unseen third man and nodded, then turned to gaze out the window. The unidentified gunman draped a wide piece of gray tape around Oriol's face and plastered it over his mouth. Then he put a small square case on the desk, unzipping it quickly. Inside was a jumble of metal implements.

The man lifted one of the implements and displayed it for him. It was a hypodermic needle and syringe—stained, used and a little corroded.

The case was full of them.

The stranger didn't bother filling the syringe with any substance. He simply stepped to Oriol's side and slammed it into his stomach. The needle went through his shirt and buried in his abdominal muscles. The next went into his biceps. The third into the fleshy skin of his throat.

The tape kept him from screaming. Oriol was shaking head to foot and the movement made the syringes bob and bounce, increasing the pain further.

The general faced him again.

"All right, give me the information I want."

Oriol looked at him wide-eyed.

"Are you army Intelligence?"

All he had to do was shake his head.

He didn't move.

The general looked out the window again; it was still early morning and Havana was starting its day.

The stranger chose another needle and syringe from the case, a particularly rusted one. Oriol wondered how many people these needles had been used on before him.

The case seemed bigger than it had at first. There could be fifty or seventy-five needles in there.

The stranger put the rusted needle in Oriol's left eye.

Joel Perin pushed the black-and-white photo across General Abello's desk. The man put down the sandwich and continued to chew reluctantly.

"When was this taken?" Abello demanded.

"Twenty minutes ago."

"Well? Who is it?"

"Agent Oriol."

Abello swallowed with difficulty. "What the hell did they do to him?"

"Tortured. Using hypodermic needles, mostly. They killed him within the past couple of hours. We got lucky—we already had a couple of their dirty-work guys under surveillance. Otherwise it might be days before we missed him. We probably never would have found him where they were taking him."

"Which was where?"

"The ocean. They had him chained and weighted."

"I see. Do we know who did this?"

"Yes. It was General Serra. Oriol was investigating Serra, as you know. I believe he found incriminating evidence that he was about to turn over to you. Serra discovered his infiltration and tortured him to find out how much he'd learned, who he worked for, all the rest."

"Would he have buckled under torture?"

Perin shrugged. "On the one hand, he would have known his life was forfeit as soon as the torture started. On the other hand, look at him."

Abello looked at the photo again. Perin knew he was considering what he—or any man—would have done if inflicted with that much pain. At some point all considerations become irrelevant except for the cessation of pain.

"The general has a man who's used this form of coercion before."

Abello nodded. "You suggest what?"

"I suggest we move immediately to take the general into custody and find out what he knows of us, who else belongs to the conspiracy, and when the conspiracy plans on making its move."

"I agree," Abello said, nodding. He hadn't stopped looking at the photo of the deceased Agent Oriol, but he did now and nailed Perin to his chair with a hard look. "Give me a percentage—your estimation of the possibility of General Serra's guilt in this murder and in belonging to the conspiracy."

Perin had worked with Abello before and had expected the question.

"Seventy percent."

Abello picked up the phone and dialed. He spoke one word and waited again.

"Minister, this is General Abello. I am making an official report." In terse, brief language Abello explained the situation—and Perin's recommendation—to the Minister of Revolutionary Armed Forces, who happened to be vice president and the brother of the president.

"Yes, Minister," Abello said finally. He paused. "Seventy percent." Seconds later he hung up the phone.

"We bring in Serra," he said.

THE SUN WAS JUST PEEKING into the small valley when General Resnikoff's car pulled into the drive in front of Manny Quinones's sprawling house. He had called the night before to warn of his impending visit.

Quinones's greeting was less than cordial.

"First of all, Resnikoff, I dislike being dictated to. I also dislike receiving calls in the middle of the night that stir up my entire family."

"I can promise you this is a real emergency, Mr. Quinones," Resnikoff replied.

"It may be an emergency for you. I doubt it will turn out to be an emergency for me."

They stood on the stone steps to the house for a moment in cold silence, then Resnikoff said, "It may not be an emergency for you, Mr. Quinones, but it most certainly is a great opportunity for you."

Quinones snorted. "We'll see. Come in."

He strode into the house with Resnikoff at his heels, and they went to the same meeting room they had used before, on the screened porch overlooking the valley. There was a chill in the morning air, but Resnikoff wasn't about to complain about it. A houseman poured coffee as the men sat, and Resnikoff sipped it hot and black.

"What's the deal?" Quinones asked sharply.

"The deal is this. You supply your men to my cause and, after we're in charge of Cuba, we give you free access to one port on the island. You'll have unrestricted use of the port. You can do as you please. Move in and out as many ships as the port can handle. The only condition is that you do not move drugs into Cuba."

Quinones sipped his own coffee and sucked on his cigarette, then leaned forward to stab it out in a clear glass ashtray. "No. This is not of interest to me."

"What? You were practically begging for the deal a few days ago."

Quinones glared at him sharply. "I think you are mistaken."

"You wanted it, surely. I know you did."

"I was interested in the deal at the time. I am not now."

"But what has changed? And why in the world would you not want the benefits of a port in Cuba, just a few hours from the Florida coast?"

"I was interested in the deal when I thought there was a

good chance of your success in this venture, General. In the past few days I've heard things are not going so well for you.''

"Where did you hear this?" Resnikoff demanded.

"It doesn't matter," Quinones said. "Your presence and your very attitude bears out the fact that your undertaking is meeting with severe difficulties. At our last meeting you were adamantly opposed to the very idea of my shipments touching Cuban shores. Now you come begging me. All for the sake of getting another fifty men added to your arsenal. That smacks of desperation.''

Quinones didn't give the Russian time to rebut.

"I do not like gambling, and I especially do not like gambling with my men. My line of business is risky enough without taking wild chances.''

"I can assure you that I am not a desperate man," Resnikoff said, sitting tall. "I am in need of more men. I have had some difficulties. You can imagine how hard it has been to put together a major infiltration force in secret, and you can imagine that there have been other parties that do not want that fighting force put together. In fact if it is desperation you're looking for, it is the desperation of my enemies.''

"Who are?" Quinones asked.

"The Cubans, certainly, and the Americans. I am sure they are not working together, but both suspect what is happening and both would rather I not succeed. And both realize that I very well might succeed, especially with the support I'm getting from the Cubans themselves.

"The people of Cuba asked for communism. Castro failed to give it to them, just as the hypocrites of the Soviet Union stole communism from the people of Russia. We have now lost Russia. But we can make of Cuba the glorious workers' paradise it was always destined to be. The paradise the people of Cuba have asked for.''

Quinones lit another cigarette and stared out over the valley. "If the people of Cuba are so willing to help you, what need have you for an army at all?''

"For the initial attack, the offensive that will cut the head of the swollen capitalist government of Cuba. Rest assured I have the means to get into the Havana palace and end the reign of the president and vice president once and for all. Once the old government is decapitated, our allies inside Cuba will launch into motion, taking out the other power players in the old government. We have surgical strikes planned in many major Cuban cities, designed to remove the Castro loyalists. Within hours the third step will fall into place—the military forces will see that there is no old regime left to follow and they will turn to us. Finally the people of the island will clamor to join our New Revolution."

"Why do you think that?"

Resnikoff leaned forward and said, almost passionately, "Because they despise Castro and the betrayal he's perpetrated."

"Really?"

"You want proof? Look at the prison system in Cuba. The island has virtually no serious crime, yet it has just about the highest prison rate in the Caribbean. Why? Without serious crime why should the police need guns? Why do most of them carry cattle prods and pepper spray, in addition to guns, as their standard equipment?

"Because the people are rebelling. Because they are fed up with the ineffectual dictator of a capitalist system that pretends to be Communist. Castro wears thousand-dollar Italian suits!"

"You think stricter totalitarianism is what the people want?" Quinones asked with a smirk.

Resnikoff stared at him. "It is what they will get," he said, his words like frozen blocks of ice that chilled the room. "I am not desperate, Mr. Quinones, and I will not ask you again. Do you want this deal or will you let it slip through your fingers? Because there are other men in Colombia at this moment who would kill for this opportunity."

Quinones nodded, smoke leaking from the corners of his mouth, stabbing out another cigarette. "We have a deal," he said. "You've got my men, Resnikoff."

The Russian stood.

"When's the big move, General?"

Resnikoff looked at his watch. "In twenty hours."

"I'd better wake the men."

"YOU DON'T THINK Fagen is going to bow out, do you?" Brognola asked.

"Tough call," Bolan said. "He's very determined. But he's suffered some substantial losses in the last day."

"Conspicuous losses," Brognola reminded him. "If he bows out now, he's lost major face."

"You think he's got reinforcements waiting in the wings?"

"No. But you know how these groups network. They're constantly restructuring and changing, and Fagen's got to have contacts and men throughout the merc underground in Central America, Mexico, even the U.S. My guess is he's calling in favors as we speak."

"We'll know soon enough," Bolan replied. "I'm five minutes from his house in Orange Walk."

"Think he's still there?"

"I'll let you know."

Bolan made quick work of replacing the original license plates, then wrapped a bulky mass of bandages around his head, ignoring the curious looks of the service station attendants. He drove the four blocks to the house owned by the American mercenary leader, blaring his horn at the gate. The sun was just coming up, scraping between the buildings without yet reaching the street level.

He leaned against the window, one arm dropped over the steering wheel as if he were barely holding on to consciousness. A guard with a hand inside his jacket walked to the gate and squinted out between the bars suspiciously. His face registered shock as he recognized the vehicle as one belonging to the Guatemalan compound.

There were shouts from inside the courtyard and the gate opened inward. Bolan allowed the vehicle to roll inside at its idle speed. He squeaked to a halt and opened the door, half falling out. The guard ran around to him, shouting in rapid-fire Spanish.

"Morning," Bolan said as the guard grabbed for him, and brought him to a halt with the 93-R pressed into his chest.

The guard jumped back and clawed for the weapon hidden inside his jacket. Bolan didn't give him the chance to free it from its holster. The 93-R coughed one time and the 9 mm round crashed into the guard's chest, sending him to the cobblestones, dead before his skull cracked against them.

Bolan ripped off the bandages and rounded the front of the 4WD, heading for the entrance to the house, which was up a flight of enclosed concrete steps. Footsteps rapped against the stairs, and the soldier quickly determined it was two men. He stepped into the stairwell and found two gunmen armed with automatic weapons. A single triburst from the 93-R downed both, and Bolan stepped out of the way to allow their bodies to roll to the cobblestones and come to a stop. A quick glance told him they needed no further attention.

Three leaps took him up the flight of stairs, where he ripped open the door to a hail of gunfire, which he ducked beneath with milliseconds to spare. He ran into the parlor behind a large wooden table and sank to the floor, where he spotted the gunman across the room, his feet visible under the legs of the furniture. He leaped up and fired once at the slightly exposed head. The 9 mm round sliced into the gunman's hairline, partially decapitating him.

Bolan bolted across the room, leveling the Beretta at a young gunner who had tossed down his gun and raised his hands high into the air.

"Where's Fagen?"

"I don't know."

Bolan gestured with the 93-R, and the young man's eyes locked on the big handgun. "You're going to the morgue unless I find out where Fagen is."

"You can't shoot me in cold blood," the youth gasped.

"Tell that to the three dead men downstairs."

"You're an American and so am I! Americans have laws."

"You agree to aid Communists intending to violently over-throw a nation neighboring the United States and now you want me to offer you the courtesy of U.S. law? Don't count on it. Tell me where Fagen is, or I'll kill you where you stand."

"I don't believe—"

Sancho yelped as a streak of hot flame ripped across his shoulder.

"You're a fucking maniac!" he screamed, trying to hold in the flood of blood pouring out of his shoulder.

"Where's Fagen? I won't ask you again."

"He left here an hour ago!"

"And he went where?"

"Belize City."

"Where in Belize City?"

"To the airport. He's got the rest of his men with him, and he's got a bunch of soldiers meeting him there. They're chartering a jet to Santo Domingo."

"From there?"

"I don't know where. All I know is that the Russians are staging everybody before the attack."

"Which is when?"

"Nineteen hours."

"What's the plan?"

"They're going to chute into the palace and take out the president and vice president. After that, their allies in the government will take out the loyalists. Then the population will fall in line."

"So it all hinges on getting into the palace. How are they planning to do that?"

"They've got inside information and help. You'll never be able to stop them. No way!"

Bolan nodded. "Then I'll die trying. And if I'm going, I want you to go with me."

A barrage of 9 mm rounds slammed into the wall and floor around Sancho and he fell onto his face, sobbing and crying. When the barrage stopped he huddled there, too horrified to move, waiting for an explosion of pain to come from whatever parts of his body had been shot. It took him a full minute to sit up and realize he hadn't been wounded further—and to find himself alone.

BROGNOLA LISTENED to Bolan's brief in silence. Then he said, "Jack's already headed to Belize City. I shipped him out just after our last call."

"Why?"

"You'll understand that after I tell you this—one of our Drug Enforcement Administration liaisons contacted us. He knew we were keeping an eye on the Quinones drug family and thought we'd want to know about a very recent surge in activity."

"What kind of activity?"

"We're not sure of that yet. But we patched into the DEA phone taps and their satellite pictures from the past hour. We know that a small commercial aircraft landed in Neiva early this morning. A chauffeured car took a single Caucasian male from the Neiva airport to the Quinones house in the country. It was the second time in the past week this same guy's met with Quinones. They fed us a picture of the guy and told us they didn't have any idea as to his identity. It took the Bear about as long as it's taking me to tell you this to ID the guy electronically."

"Ex-KGB?" Bolan suggested.

"Yeah. A general named Resnikoff."

"So now we have a name for the guy in charge."

"The next would-be dictator of Cuba," Brognola growled.

"Then what?"

"Resnikoff and Quinones meet for about ten minutes. Then Resnikoff leaves and the next thing you know the place is going ape-shit. Everybody's getting their act together and packing off to the airport."

"How many?"

"Forty-five men."

"What kind of aircraft?"

"That's where it gets confusing. They got on a commercial flight to Nassau."

Bolan considered that. "There's a piece missing here. All Fagen's mercs have moved out, too, but they're headed for Santo Domingo."

Brognola sighed. "Are these guys all going on vacation or what?"

"They've got to be getting their act together somewhere. And neither the Bahamas or the Hispaniola offer a convenient jumping-off point for a Havana hard probe."

"Not much does outside of Key West."

"Right. What do we have in terms of intelligence-gathering in Santo Domingo and Nassau?" Bolan asked.

"The DEA's got enough manpower to watch for our arriving armies and observe what kind of flights they transfer to."

"Good. Meanwhile, I'll meet Grimaldi in Belize City. I hope he's piloting something fast-moving."

"Yeah. I'll get you wherever you might need to go, anyway."

Bolan looked at his watch. Less than nineteen hours remained until the attack was staged to occur against the government of Cuba. In less than one day a new radical Communist nation might been born virtually within earshot of the U.S., which just might have access to nuclear weapons.

THE LEARJET 31 WAS a twin-engine plane that nosed to a quick stop on the tarmac in Belize City. Bolan stood by as the portable steps were wheeled into place and a thin figure opened the door from the inside.

Bolan waved and grabbed his pack. "Taxi."

"Very funny," Grimaldi said. "Do I have time to soak up some rays, maybe grab a piña colada on the beach?"

"That's a negative," Bolan said, mounting the stairs and taking Grimaldi's hand firmly. "We're counting the hours right now. We've got to get airborne immediately."

Grimaldi sighed and shrugged. "Ah, well. Maybe when this

is all over with we can come back. I have several favorite bars and women in this city."

"I don't doubt it."

The jet was the type typically flown by highly paid corporate executives. It was well-appointed, luxurious when compared to the Sea Stallion Bolan had bailed out of recently, and, in fact, when compared to most of the aircraft he typically found Grimaldi piloting. It had a wingspan just under forty-four feet and was powered by a pair of Garrett TFE 731-2-3B turbofans. It had passenger seating for ten, but Bolan installed himself in the copilot's seat and Grimaldi radioed for clearance to take off again.

"Next stop?"

"I was hoping you knew," Bolan said. "Just get airborne and I'll get on the horn to the Farm. They should have a destination determined for us."

Grimaldi grimaced. "Is there a general direction, at least?"

Bolan pointed vaguely northeast. "That way."

"Great."

Within minutes they were off the tarmac, and the world beneath them changed from brown and green to beautiful, sunny blue. Bolan patched through to Stony Man Farm and a familiar female voice came through his headset.

"Morning," said Barbra Price, mission controller at the Farm. "How's the weather in the Caribbean?"

"It's been a little stormy," Bolan said. "At least what I've seen of it. What I'm wondering is where I go next. Our pilot friend would like some coordinates by which to steer this pretty plane you supplied him with."

Bolan could almost hear the smile in Price's voice when she replied. "Don't mock our airplane. It's fast, it lands on a dime and it doesn't provoke half the attention a U.S. Navy jet would elicit. As a matter of fact, we've just got word from our DEA contacts in Nassau. They watched our Colombian friends come through customs. Apparently there were a lot of them and they bogged down the customs process for quite a while. Really angered a bunch of vacationers from Vancouver who were trying to get at the beach as fast as possible."

"That's too bad. So the Colombians are on Grand Bahama Island?"

"No. But they had to go through customs because they didn't transfer to another commercial flight. They piled onto a chartered DC-9."

"Chartered to where?"

"Key West."

Bolan felt a moment's frustration. "They can't be going to Key West. I'm sure it'll show up there empty."

"I'm sure you're right. But now that we've got tabs on it we can watch it via satellite. The Colombians will almost certainly parachute in to wherever they're going. Their options for landing a DC-9 between Nassau and Key West are severely limited."

"Right."

Grimaldi, monitoring on the headphones, chimed in. "Striker and I will continue northeast over the Yucatán Channel, then turn due east. You can give us more precise directions as they become available."

"Right," Price said. "Striker, when's the last time you slept?"

Bolan considered it. "It's been a while."

"Might as well catch a few winks while you can."

BOLAN'S EYES OPENED instantly at Grimaldi's call over the jet's loudspeaker, and he searched for his watch. He'd taken in a few hours of much-needed rest in one of the comfortable reclining passenger seats.

"We've got a target, Striker."

Bolan appeared in the cockpit a moment later. "What is it?"

"Cay Zucar," Grimaldi said, handing him a laminated aeronautical map and indicating a tiny dot that appeared to be about one hundred miles northeast of Havana.

"Another private island?" Bolan asked.

"Yeah. Owned by a Florida millionaire who seldom uses it and whose whereabouts have been confirmed in Miami. But communication with the staff on the island has been lost."

"The Russians have taken over by force." Bolan nodded. "They've probably depended on it as their contingency plan from the outset. I forced their hand when I rendered their Reunion Island base unusable."

"I guess you did. The communications have been lost within just the past few hours, and the DC-9 did a direct fly-over before heading straight for Key West. The satellite pictures confirmed they parachuted in. Those poor Colombian drug-runners probably messed their drawers, going in like that. I don't think it's in their typical job profile."

"I'm afraid you're going to be left out of the excitement again," Bolan stated.

"I know it, damn it," Grimaldi said.

"Maybe you can get the okay to head back to Belize City for some R and R."

"No way, Striker. I'm dropping you off and heading straight for the Keys myself. I'll swap this businessman-special and stand ready with a helo for your extraction. By the way, you need to phone home—they've arranged for you to have some backup, even if it's not me."

"That's right," Price was saying less than a minute later. "We called a SEAL team out of Guantánamo. It should be arriving at the meet coordinates about ten minutes ahead of you with a landing raft that'll get you to the island unadvertised."

"Good."

"There it is," Grimaldi said, pointing out the window as a tiny green dot appeared in the distance and far to the south. Bolan could make out no features. They couldn't risk a closer approach that might alert the inhabitants of their coming.

He clapped Grimaldi on the shoulder and headed into the back of the jet to make his jump.

"I'M SLOW AND LOW," Grimaldi said over the loudspeaker. "Go when you're ready. The SEALs have a marker out for you."

Bolan opened the hatch, setting off an alarm in the cabin. The jet wasn't intended to be used for skydiving. He spotted the floating marker deployed by the SEAL team and ejected the large pack provided by Stony Man Farm. It contained a small satellite dish that would allow him to link with the Farm. An instant later he leaped out after it.

Above him, the jet raced away, veering north.

For a long minute the world was quiet, filled only with the rushing of the wind as Bolan descended almost peacefully into the sea.

12

Maria Rodriguez looked up and saw what amounted to a platoon of army soldiers pour from the elevator and the stairway and deploy throughout the office. A man without a uniform appeared at her desk from out of nowhere, as she was standing quickly to her feet, and presented identification and placed an urgent finger across her lips.

She was so startled she didn't really see the insignia on the identification and she said, "Who are you? What is happening?"

"Sit down and be very quiet, please, *señorita*," Agent Perin said. It was then Rodriguez noticed a man with a DGA general's insignia approaching behind the plainclothesman. She sat at her desk and watched them in silence.

The soldiers were armed, and they moved about the office with a purpose Rodriguez didn't understand, moving gradually closer and closer to her desk, like a noose drawing tighter, but continually covering the floor, as if they were nervous.

The plainclothes agent and the DGA general knocked on General Serra's door. Should she have alerted the general over the intercom?

Two of the soldiers flanked the agent and the general, handguns drawn.

The agent opened the door and the four of them entered the office, followed by several soldiers.

There was a shout, and a heavy sound like a body hitting the floor. Rodriguez wanted to get up and run to the door of the general's office, but it was now crowded with soldiers. She heard the general swearing and cursing. She heard the agent declare loudly, "General Serra, you are under arrest."

They led the general out in handcuffs. Rodriguez stood, finally, as the soldiers, the DGA general and the agent walked the general, head bowed, to the stairs.

A moment later the soldiers had dissipated and the hall was empty. Rodriguez sat at her desk in numb shock. Her boss, a general in the Cuban army, had just been arrested.

Now what was she supposed to do?

"WHAT'S YOUR RANK, sir?"

"Just call me Belasko," Bolan said.

The four SEALs exchanged glances.

"We were told you'd be presenting us with our orders."

Bolan looked at the young man. "We're going to make an amphibious approach on Cay Zucar. How much have you been told?"

"To expect a heavy population of well-armed Russians on the island," the SEAL team leader said.

"That's only part of the problem. By the time we get there the island will see the arrival of approximately forty soldiers supplied by a Colombian drug cartel. There will also be an unknown number of mercenary soldiers joining them."

"Sounds like they're preparing an invasion."

"They are," Bolan said, checking his watch. "Within sixteen hours they're going to attempt to infiltrate and assassinate the executive officials of Communist Cuba and put in place a new totalitarian government." There were whistles of amazement around the small raft. "There is plenty of dislike for Castro on the streets of Cuba. Things have gone downhill there, despite the legalization of limited capitalism. There are plenty of people with plenty of power in Castro's government who have already thrown in with the new Communists. There are plenty more who will join the New Revolution once they see the way the wind is blowing. Needless to say, the United States isn't in favor of seeing a new Communist state formed to replace the old one. Especially one with access to a lot of

Soviet hardware, probably including Soviet nuclear capability."

"What're we going to do about it?" the team leader asked. "Seems we're a little undermanned to do battle."

"You're right. The U.S. can't do much. Officially Castro won't even acknowledge what's going on, although he knows about it well enough and is, I'm sure, working on putting a halt to it at his own end. Personally I don't have a lot of confidence in the DGA to weed out the revolutionaries. Even if they were able to locate a full fifty percent of the sympathizers in the upper echelons of the Cuban military, it wouldn't be enough. Once the momentum of the revolution is built, it'll be a freight train without brakes. Nothing will stop it until it has run its course. Our goal is to stop that train before it even starts rolling out of the station. Got it?"

"Yeah. But how?"

Bolan gestured to the empty horizon to the west. "I think— I hope—that the Russians have assembled most of their hardware and nearly all their men on Cay Zucar. If we can get in and plant enough explosives to render most of it useless, they'll be crippled. If we cripple them bad enough, the engine will never start revving." Bolan nodded to the tarpaulin-covered pile of gear in the rear of the raft. "I assume that's the explosives I requested."

The SEAL team leader gave him an enthusiastic grin. "Sir, we've got enough explosives to blow Cay Zucar off the map."

Bolan's mouth became a hard line. "That's what I wanted to hear."

THE ZODIAC RAFT SAT almost invisible on the dark water, still Bolan ordered them to anchor it well off the island to avoid getting spotted if the ex-KGBers had thought to set up a guard to watch for an assault. Chances were they were expecting a large-scale attack or none at all.

The team had been deployed with a SEAL Delivery Vehicle Mark VIII, which had been tethered under the raft and allowed them to make the approach to the island with a significant load of gear without exhausting themselves. BUD/S graduates or not, a swim several miles long would leave anyone tired, especially with the pounds they were dragging. But the long, black submerged Mark VIII propelled them and their gear to the island with almost no effort on their part.

At a distance of twenty yards from shore the team parked the Mark VIII and waited while their team leader scanned the shore. Utilizing their famous LAR V rebreathing apparatus, the team left no bubbles on the surface of the water and sat invisible offshore. The team leader broke the surface with just his field glasses. After ten minutes he turned and gave them the okay signal. Bolan took the lead then, and the team made landfall quickly. Although the shore was mostly beach he chose a rocky point for emergence, and strained to hear the sound of a guard during the few most dangerous moments when the men were exposed. After two minutes the shore was empty again. The water the men had tracked onto the rocks began evaporating instantly, and soon there was no sign of their landing.

The SEALs instantly began to establish a base camp of sorts, stripping their wet-suit gear in favor of brown-and-green camou outfits, unloading guns and explosives from their waterproofing, and hiding their landing gear for later reuse, all in near silence. Each man carried a .45-caliber OHS, the newest handgun in the SEAL arsenal, as well as a Type 56-2, a Chinese automatic weapon that was essentially an AK-47 copy with some design upgrades effective in a short-range firefight, but it would make a hell of a racket in the process.

Bolan unloaded the portable satellite station the Farm had provided, erecting it in bushes where it would best resist detection. He oriented it carefully and switched on the portable power pack that came with it. It would operate for hours.

He quietly impressed on the men the need for silence, although he was sure they understood its importance already. They were five men. No matter how dangerously they were armed, they would be in deep trouble if they were found out on an island full of enemies.

"Remember our priorities," he stated. "At the top of the list is the runway and all vertical takeoff equipment, especially the Forger if it's here. Next is the offensive hardware. Guns, missiles, whatever they've got. Finally we need to take out their communications capability."

The SEALs understood his directives. The team started its swift, silent march through the palm trees and scant undergrowth of the cay.

Bolan hadn't partaken of the smorgasbord of hardware the SEALs offered. He chose in these circumstances to stick with the M-16 A-1/M-203, for which the SEALs had provided a backpack containing a generous supply of spare mags and a variety of grenades. He also chose to stick with the suppressed Beretta 93-R.

Although Bolan hadn't discussed them with his SEAL team, there were two possible scenarios in which they might be able to make use of their assault rifles without giving themselves away, both contingent on the fact that the Russians would probably be engaged in heavy training to familiarize their most recent recruits with the following day's pattern of attack. One: the enemy had issued blanks for battle-simulation—the real gunfire could be hidden in the blank fire. Two: the recruits were training for their battle insertion, meaning they'd be in the air and out of the fight.

Bolan hoped for, but wouldn't count on, the latter.

The SEAL team moved through the undergrowth with a quiet skill that came from intense training. The soldier knew these men didn't have the jungle-war experience he did, but they had lived through BUD/S training, which was enough to break any but the most dedicated soldier, and were experienced in insertion and removal exercises. There was little more he could ask for in a commodity warrior.

At the same time Bolan knew well enough that every soldier was an individual, with individual strengths and weaknesses, skill and talent. Ideally he would have liked to know these men better before participating in a hard probe with them, thus know what to expect of them in battle.

The SEALs came to a halt a split second after Bolan stopped moving. They had all detected movement ahead—a flash of motion through the trees. Standing stock-still in the undergrowth for a long moment, they heard the shouts of men and the rumble of an engine of some kind. At Bolan's signal they proceeded. Where the trees ended and the sun reached the ground, the grasses and bushes became more dense, and here the team came to a halt.

Bolan took a quick inventory. He spotted the second Yak Forger parked at the far end of the giant clearing, which was at least two miles long and sliced in two by a concrete runway. Parked near the VTOL fighter plane was the tiny, windowless robot prop plane marked with Cyrillic characters. A giant Russian Antonov An-32 light tactical transport plane was also present, its twin Ivchenko AI-20M engines rumbling in idle. A group of approximately eighty were circled around it, getting some type of instruction. A team of what Bolan took to be officers in a Russian four-wheel-drive desert vehicle watched from several yards away.

The north end of Cay Zucar opened into a harbor, too shallow to allow in any but the smallest watercraft. Twenty rubber rafts were parked on the narrow, sandy beach, while out in the ocean a variety of Russian watercraft were at anchor, the Soviet insignia on the sides carelessly spray-painted over and still discernible, even from a distance.

Beyond the Forger, on the rocky eastern side of the island, was a single wharf. A Cuban navy vessel was anchored there, and a group of four Cuban officers approached.

A SECOND CAR WAS SENT to the wharf, and Resnikoff waited as it picked up the Cubans and approached, coming to a halt nearby. As he stepped down from his own vehicle to greet them, Resnikoff realized some of the faces were unfamiliar.

"Where's General Serra?" he asked by way of greeting.

"I had him arrested," General Abello said.

"You what?"

"You heard me. As I told you, the minister ordered me to

put agents in the field to investigate the rumors of our plot. So I did."

"And you allowed them to find out about Serra?"

"Listen, Resnikoff, I have been doing a very uncomfortable balancing act. I had to come up with a credible strategy for uncovering the truth about the plot. The minister insisted I put some of my best agents in the field, and he wanted detailed progress reports. He's not taking the rumors lightly. I did my best to downplay the situation without making him suspicious of me."

"So instead you sacrificed Serra."

"I warned Serra my agents would be on to him. He over-reacted when one of them broke into his office. The man didn't even uncover anything incriminating. But Serra had him killed anyway. One of the other agents found out about it, and I couldn't keep the report from reaching the minister. So I had no choice but to have Serra arrested."

"Where is he now?" Resnikoff demanded.

"In jail. Where do you think?"

"Being questioned?"

"Yes, but I was able to stall the start of the questioning and it hasn't become intense yet. We'll simply make freeing him one of our first orders of business."

Resnikoff shrugged, then looked pointedly at the unfamiliar faces.

"Allow me to introduce General Alejandro Marquez, who we can count on to serve as our army liaison."

"I assure you, I can make myself a benefit to the New Revolution, General Resnikoff," Marquez said self-confidently.

"This is General Jordi Crespin," General Ricardo Mazon said, "who I have told you about. He is our new navy liaison."

Crespin took a half step forward and nodded crisply, but kept his eyes on Resnikoff every second. "You can count on me as well, General. I've been waiting for an opportunity such as this my entire career."

"Haven't we all," Mazon said.

Resnikoff shook his head. "Two of our staunchest supporters are out of the game—it's not good. Solas dead and Serra in jail. One on top of our other troubles. We're lucky we have the manpower and the contacts to proceed."

"But we are proceeding?" Mazon asked.

"Definitely. If we can count on our new generals to come through with the diversions we need?"

Marquez and Crespin gave their assurances.

"Then let's review our strategy."

THE SEAL TEAM LEADER led his men back through the undergrowth and carefully watched for signs of patrols on the west shore of the island. The place looked as vacant as it had when they landed an hour earlier. Quickly they outfitted themselves in their gear, crossed the open ground and entered the ocean. In their element, they were invisible.

In the dark water they began circling to the north.

Bolan waited until the SEAL team was on its way, then began a slow march through the woods around the perimeter of the open area, careful to stay far enough from the grass and bush of the perimeter to avoid movement that might be spotted.

There was no way he could know that he had already been spotted by a single electronic eye miles above him.

THE SATELLITE HAD BEEN deployed to automatically feed visual imagery to Soviet Intelligence stations, though now, with the end of the cold war, it had become a less vital piece of equipment. Its Moscow computer command center now followed a repetitive pattern, directing it to view various North and Central American targets at regular intervals throughout the day.

Alexander Platovsek's position had once been one of importance. This day it was less so. Although his information was used to keep an eye on the Americans, the fear of the

Americans was much less than it had been. The task had become mundane—until Platovsek was contacted by an old friend from the former KGB, General Ivan Resnikoff. Then things became more interesting.

Carefully he had programmed the satellite to perform extra functions that the Russian military Intelligence never knew about. The thermal images were taken during brief intervals, during periods in which the satellite indicated it was changing position from one target to another. The interludes were seconds long and went unnoticed by the operators. The thermal images were digitized and sent through secret phone lines out of the Moscow office without ever registering in the command computer system.

Platovsek liked the idea he was helping his friend Resnikoff. Once Resnikoff's revolution had succeeded, he was hoping to retire to Cuba, live the good life, sell a few secrets to the burgeoning new Communist nation.

The satellite acted so automatically that Platovsek needed to do nothing to maintain it. The operators at Resnikoff's end received the information without his involvement at all.

ONE OF RESNIKOFF'S trusted aides knocked and entered the room quickly, concern on his face. "General, we have intruders," he said in Russian.

The Russian sat up quickly and directed the aide to present the information. The aide placed two color printouts on the table, instantly recognizable as thermal images coming from the Russian satellite he had accessed, and which was proving invaluable in this undertaking. Now it had proved its worth again.

The first photo was taken at 15:33. It showed Cay Zucar as a mass of black with gray shadows. Red shapes clearly marked men and operating equipment. A tiny mass of red dots could be seen in the midst of the blackness that was the wild areas of the island.

The next printout was labeled 15:40 and showed those same red dots, now grouped on the perimeter of the clearing.

"When's our next feed?"

"Not until sixteen hundred hours, General."

Resnikoff explained the problem to the Cubans. "This is what I want you to do," he said to his aide. "Put extra guards on all the perimeter buildings and equipment. Have them report as if for a shift change, but don't allow any of the other guards to leave. Make it look casual. I want to flush them out, so we can't tip our hand. I'm sure these are the same men who have been harassing our friends in Guatemala and Mexico. Probably the same ones who killed our good friends General Solas and Major Rifkin. It would be a great relief to know they've been neutralized as a threat before we begin our operation tomorrow."

The aide left and returned when the next image was available. The guards were in place, but the intruders had changed their targets. Now only one man was left on the clearing perimeter, circling southeast, probably out to disable the Forger. A group of three or four men was heading back to the west shore of the island.

The 16:11 image showed one intruder still on the perimeter, probably waiting for a chance to attack. The four others had disappeared from the image.

"They're in the water," Crespin stated.

Resnikoff agreed. "There's no chance they are DGA, is there?"

"No. Unless I've greatly misjudged the faith the minister has in me and has initiated an intelligence operation behind my back. But I don't think so."

"Then they are U.S. That means a SEAL team," Crespin said.

Resnikoff got to his feet at once. "They're probably trying to booby-trap our ships. I want all the ships alerted. Have depth charges prepared, but tell them to keep the level of activity on the ships low. I don't want our intruders to know they're in danger." Resnikoff turned to Crespin. "If they went into the ocean within the last ten minutes, how long will it take them to reach the first ship?"

Crespin considered it. "They'll use some sort of underwater vehicle, maybe an Eight Boat, to get in as close as they can. But they won't want to get close enough for it to be detected. I'd guess they'll reach the northwesternmost point of the island, then swim in. They'll be invisible from the surface because they'll have LAR V rebreathing apparatus. I'd say they'd reach the middle of the bay in fifteen more minutes."

Resnikoff nodded and strode to the window to peer out into the bay. He pointed to the farthest of the small gunboats. "Have that ship move out to sea at least a couple of miles and then circle back. I want to start dropping depth charges about three hundred meters out in fifteen minutes, then move to the shore in seventy-five-meter increments. At the same time we'll drop charges from the nearest gunship on the east end, also moving in seventy-five-meter increments. They'll surface, dead or alive."

"What about him?" Abello asked, tapping the tiny red dot that indicated a man was hiding along the southeast perimeter of the clearing, within a stone's throw of where the Colombians were receiving their instruction.

Resnikoff looked out the window in that direction. He could see the area where the man was hidden.

"He's not going anywhere without our knowing it. My guess is he'll panic when he sees his companions bob to the surface. Deploy twelve men around the island shore." He gave his aide a hard glance. "Make them my personal guard. They should stay in constant communication. When he makes a break for it, let the men know at once. They should avoid killing him, if possible. I'd like to find out who's behind all our difficulties." He turned to the Cuban generals gathered around his meeting table. "Wouldn't you?"

13

Bolan was almost instantly suspicious of the guards' behavior. There had been four Russians gathered at the jet and another two at the robot prop plane, then four and two more respectively had joined them as if for a shift change. But the first shift had failed to leave its post.

They were chatting among themselves, smoking cigarettes, kidding around, but the casual air was forced. Their eyes scanned the palm trees and wild sugarcane and grasses one too many times for his liking.

Had the probe been discovered?

It was entirely feasible. Even a warrior skilled in jungle combat couldn't sneak past passive motion detectors and invisible perimeter gates using minuscule lasers. Who knew what the Russians had brought with them?

But so far the guards weren't coming after him. No contingent had entered the forest at any point to run him down. Bolan was confident he could make himself undetectable to all but the most skilled hunters in the forest.

There was a surge in activity aboard one of the Russian gunboats. It pulled up its anchor and sped out into the ocean, then made a long, wide turn and headed back to the island from the northwest.

Bolan had a bad feeling about it.

THE SEAL TEAM divided up the packs of explosives. Buoyed with air bladders, the packs were big and awkward if not heavy. But they were SEALs, trained to navigate in the water with heavy loads of equipment. The water was their natural habitat.

But a dangerous habitat, sometimes.

They swam away from the island until they reached seas with a depth of about twenty-five feet, deep enough to be hidden from the surface, and began to make their way to the parked Russian gunboats.

The SEAL leader paused and with a gesture brought the team to a sudden halt. He detected the approach of a boat, which slowed to a crawl a good distance away.

Was the ship looking for the SEAL team? Did they have any way of knowing the team was even there, let alone its location?

The team leader's doubts turned to horror when the first depth charge turned the ocean to churning chaos.

BOLAN'S DOUBTS DISSIPATED the instant the first depth charge went off and the sea's surface erupted. A moment later another ship to the northeast set off a charge.

Both boats were moving slowly across the wide bay, then turned and cut across it. More depth charges were dropped.

The Russians knew the SEAL team was there, and were trying to drive them to shore or blast them to pieces in the water.

Bolan watched, helpless. There was absolutely nothing he could do to save those men. Despite their skill and extensive training, he doubted there was anything they could do to save themselves.

Blast after blast echoed across the tiny island, and the surface of the bay transformed from a dark blue to a muddy brown.

The two gunboats finally started to reach shallow water. They set off four charges in rapid succession.

Bolan heard shouts and cheers from the men on the shore. One after another, four broken human shapes floated to the surface of the bay.

They died in battle. They died doing their duty. Bolan

would grieve for those men later. At the moment he noticed an opportunity.

Every man in the clearing had stopped what they were doing to watch the activity in the ocean.

He knew he was taking a wild chance. Before him, though, were two very effective weapons that needed to be disabled. He couldn't afford to pass up the opportunity. He raced into the open, crossed to the robot prop plane, paused long enough to ascertain if the Forger guards were still looking away and bolted across the open grass to the VTOL jet. Grimacing with the strain of achieving speed and silence, he stepped up the rungs to the cockpit, activated the explosives and the detonator and tucked them in place behind the pilot's seat.

He sped to ground again and double-timed it back to the robot aircraft.

"Hey!"

The jig was up and the guards turned together. Instantly there was a barrage of fire that went wide—the men knew better than to direct fire at their own plane. Bolan jumped on the wing and dragged the M-16 A-1/M-203 from his shoulder. He leveled it over the top of the aircraft and triggered one high explosive grenade, then another before pulling back behind the body of the plane for protection. The two 40 mm HE rounds exploded in the midst of the nearby guards as two of the smartest of them turned to flee. They didn't get far and the concussion blasted all four of them. Bolan hopped down from the wing of the robot plane and sent another blast in the direction of the Forger, where the eight guards were firing at him—some no longer giving consideration to damaging the robot plane. The HE grenade landed short and exploded as it hit the ground, sending sandy soil up in a cloud and obscuring the guards for a few short seconds.

Bolan didn't stand a chance against the sheer number of men within gunning distance and he knew it, speeding for the cover of the jungle as fast as he could. He leaped for the grass and wild sugarcane as the guards at the Forger got their bearings and began to fire ceaselessly into the growth, chopping it up with 5.45 mm rounds from their AK-74s. Bolan tucked himself behind the trunk of a palm tree and felt the impact of several rounds against the hard wood, stepping out from behind it as soon as the volleys of fire paused. The robot plane was out of sight now, but he relied on his memory to steer the M-203 as he triggered another HE round, then another. When the second 40 mm grenade exploded he clearly heard the crack of the fuselage. One of the guards had to have slapped in a fresh magazine and in the next instant another volley of fire chopped into the jungle.

There was a shout. "After him. Get him!"

Bolan decided sticking around was no longer wise, and he melted into the jungle. As he fell back, the image of the four SEALs floating lifelessly on the surface of the water flashed through his head.

There would be payback for those deaths, if it was the last thing he did.

The Executioner wasn't the type to let the death of good warriors go unavenged.

RESNIKOFF WATCHED the robot plane tip slowly onto its right wing. A gush of fuel poured from the broken rear end, bursting into flame and cracking the fuselage in two. The guards were giving it wide berth as they stomped into the jungle.

"Get the Forger into the air. Where's the damned pilot?" he shouted. His aide grabbed the phone, punched two quick numbers, then shouted, "Get the jet up! The general's orders!"

BOLAN PAUSED the first chance he got and took the remote control from his pocket, stabbing quickly at the illuminated red button. The explosion he expected didn't come, and he knew he was out of range. He tucked the device back in his pocket and continued through the trees, the crash of footsteps less than thirty yards behind him.

He increased his speed, leaving an obvious trail of floral

wreckage, then veered to the left and decreased his sped substantially in order to leave a virtually invisible trail. The sudden decrease in his progress brought the gunners close behind him and at least one man passed within several strides of him—but the man proceeded to the southeast while Bolan went northwest. The men would reach the southern shore of the island in just minutes and hopefully assume Bolan was fleeing along the shoreline. By heading directly through the jungle he would reach his landing point minutes ahead of them.

"WHERE ARE YOU NOW?" Resnikoff demanded into the walkie-talkie.

"We've almost reached the south shore," the guard responded. "Tell our men on the shore to watch for him. He's got to come out somewhere."

"Shore patrol, did you hear that?"

"Yes, but we haven't seen him."

Resnikoff issued an expletive. "Well, he hasn't left the island! He'd got to be somewhere!" He grabbed the mike from a radio set on the desk and shouted for the Forger pilot. "Where are you, damn it?"

The Forger was airborne over the jungle, the pilot searching in the places where the trees thinned. He accelerated and passed over the guards. "Heading southwest, and I've just passed over our search patrol. I'm not seeing him either, Base."

"THIS OUGHT TO HELP," Resnikoff's aide said, handing him two more thermal images. The first was from minutes earlier, just before the mayhem occurred. The second was less than a minute old. The tiny red pinpricks that was the search patrol could clearly be spotted marching through the palm trees. One red spot was situated in the middle of the forest, far to the search patrol's left.

"He evaded you!" Resnikoff shouted into the walkie-talkie

he held in his other hand. "He's almost in the direct center of the island, probably still headed northwest. Shore patrol on the west side of the island, be ready for him! Search patrol, go northwest, repeat, northwest!" He put the walkie-talkie on the table and grabbed the mike for the Yak. "Get that aircraft over the middle of the island and head northwest. He's evaded our search party, and he's probably trying to get into the water on the western shore."

"I've got it!" the Forger pilot exclaimed.

"Get all the men we've got and send them into the jungle, southwest of this building. Spread them out! We'll net him! The island is too small for him to escape."

Resnikoff felt the eyes of the other generals on him. They were watching the commotion calmly, with little to add. Resnikoff felt suddenly foolish for allowing one man to elicit so much confusion from his operation.

"You see him yet?" he demanded into the radio.

"Just arriving at the center of the island," the jet pilot said. "I don't see him yet."

"When you spot him, you nail him, got it?"

"Yes. I'll take him out."

Resnikoff's eyes fell on the other thermal image, sitting ignored on the desk. It was taken from just seconds before the confusion had started.

He tried to spot the intruder. Where had the bastard been? He wasn't at the jungle perimeter.

There he was—at the Forger! The guards were all several paces away, and the intruder had made his way all the way to the jet before being discovered. What had he done during those few furtive seconds?

Resnikoff's heart jumped in his throat and he grabbed the mike.

"Forger pilot, this is Resnikoff—"

"I see him, Base!"

"Get back to the base right now! That's an order!"

"I see him, Base! I can nail him!"

"No—I repeat! Return to base immediately. You are rigged to explode!"

BOLAN HEARD THE ROAR of the slow-moving aircraft as it moved across the jungle a hundred yards behind him and he veered into an area of thin growth, bringing himself in full view of the Forger. The aircraft adjusted in flight to fire at him.

Bolan veered into the thick overgrowth and threaded back to the Forger. The jet hovered twenty feet above the roof of palm trees as the pilot looked for him.

The soldier grabbed at the remote for the detonator and pressed the red lighted button. There was no response, and he ran through the trees to the Forger's position until he emerged from under a great spreading palm to stare directly up at the belly of the huge black metal beast.

He saw the Forger tilt suddenly and the pilot looked directly down at him, his face clearly conveying his sudden terror. Somehow he knew. Bolan didn't stop to consider this strange turn of events. He withdrew the remote control device again and held it directly above his head.

The pilot fed a sudden burst of fuel to the lifters and the hovering jet tried to thrust itself directly into the sky, ascending just five feet before Bolan pressed the button on the remote control device.

The explosive shattered the cockpit, killing the pilot instantly and rending the controls of the Yak to scrap metal. The thruster fire wavered, and the Yak flipped itself into an out-of-control somersault before plummeting into the jungle in a ball of flame that hit the ground, cracked and exploded.

Bolan had already started to run, west, making a direct line for the ocean, now his only safe haven. The tremor of the explosion reached him, and he rode it out during his run.

A moment later he reached the shore and stopped. To his left he spotted a guard, staring in amazement at the magnificent tongues of flame from the middle of the island. No one else was in sight.

Bolan had only waterproofing for the 93-R. He tucked the M-16 A-1/M-203 under a mulch of fallen palm leaves, then crawled among the rocks from the trees to the ocean, slithering into the sea like an amphibious eel.

The swim was tiring, and he hung to the side of the black
rubber Zodiac raft for five minutes, resting. That was all the
time he had before he heard the approaching thrum of a
gunboat.

The slate-gray craft was traveling at twenty miles per hour
when it spotted the raft and approached. Bolan stayed low and
hid behind the raft. The Russian boat was about twenty-five
feet in length with a wide, low windshield and high-mounted
.50-caliber machine gun at the rear. He grabbed a lungful of
air before submerging and swimming to the rear of the Russian
vessel as it came to a halt. He broke the surface as silently as
possible and grabbed a handhold, coming up almost directly
behind one of the crew. Two others were on board, one piloting the craft, another contacting Cay Zucar on the radio.

"It doesn't look like it, Base. The raft's empty. No, not
even a radio. Yes, all right."

Bolan pulled himself up and kneeled on a narrow shelf provided on the exterior of the craft, using the rear man to shield
his presence from the others. With a swift movement he helped
himself to the Russian's hip-mounted Makarov, with the other
hand jerking the man backward into the sea.

The man shouted and splashed into the water. Bolan targeted the radioman first, who was turning in alarm. The shot
dropped him to the deck with a thump. The next shot cored
the pilot, who staggered to his feet as if to try to wrestle the
gun from Bolan's hand. A second shot took him down.

Bolan stepped inside the boat and turned the Makarov on

its former owner. The swimmer sobbed once, coughing up seawater. Bolan fired before the man had a chance to beg for mercy. The body went limp and floated to the surface in a dark puddle that began to spread in the ocean.

He wasted no time in dumping the others into the sea, then shot the raft several times. It instantly began to deflate and bubble in the water.

GENERAL ABELLO FOUND Agent Joel Perin waiting for him at his office when he arrived in the evening.

"What is it?" he asked as he seated himself at his desk. Perin, coming in behind him, shut the door.

"General Serra has implicated several others in the conspiracy. Here is the list."

Abello took the list as if he were taking a lit firecracker and scanned it quickly.

What he saw pleased him.

He read it more thoroughly. There had to be fourteen names on the list, all generals in the local command. The more Abello read the more he wanted to laugh. That Serra was a good man. He had carefully implicated precisely all the wrong people: all the people who would most steadfastly oppose any change in leadership in Cuba; all the men, to be blunt, who might hinder the New Revolution.

"You are sure of these names?"

"I went over all those names with General Serra very thoroughly, General Abello. The general was…cooperative once he started to talk. He is trying to earn a light punishment for himself, I think."

"Indeed, he ought to get it if all these men are guilty. This is a great breakthrough. Just think of all the damage these men might be able to do. These are some of the most powerful men in Cuba, Joel! If we can stop them in their tracks, all at one time, we can save the people of Cuba incalculable trouble."

Perin nodded.

Abello studied the list a moment longer.

"I'm calling the minister," he declared and grabbed the phone.

He dialed a number and said, "Abello, here, where's the minister?"

"He's at dinner," the secretary replied.

"I need to speak to him immediately."

"He's at dinner with his brother."

Abello wanted to laugh. More fortuitous still. "This is an emergency. Please patch me through at once."

There was a click and another ring, and the phone was picked up without greeting. "This is General Abello of the DGA. I need to speak to the minister immediately. This is an emergency."

There was silence and Abello said to Perin, "The minister is at dinner with the president."

Perin was slightly alarmed when he heard that. He would never have dreamed of interrupting the president and his brother at dinner.

But the situation called for it. General Abello was right. If all those traitors could be stopped now, before they did any real damage, catastrophe might be averted.

"Yes, Minister," Abello said, "I assure you it is an emergency. I have in my office Agent Joel Perin. He has presented me with a list of names I think would be very interesting to you."

Abello succinctly explained about the investigation and death of Agent Oriol, the arrest of General Serra and the confession Serra had made just that afternoon.

"If I may offer my suggestion, Minister, it is this—I would like to put Agent Perin in charge of a task force consisting of several top Intelligence agents and military police to stage simultaneous arrests of every man on this list. My feeling is that the sooner we remove these men from their positions of power the less damage they can do. Who knows? They may be ready to strike now."

Perin allowed the words to echo in his head—himself in

charge of one of the most important operations in the agency's history!

"Yes, most are in Havana. The rest are accessible."

The conversation continued for several minutes between the general and the minister, and Perin heard little of it, his head swimming with the momentous nature of what was happening.

Then Abello hung up the phone.

"Do it, Agent Perin. You have full presidential authority to bring every man on this list into custody."

"What if Serra lied, though, General? What if some of these men are loyal?"

"They'll be fairly judged, of course. We're not going to rely on Serra's testimony alone. But we can't take the chance of leaving them in their positions if they are traitors. Some of them might be offended. But—" Abello shrugged "—let them complain to the president and the vice president if they wish. Begin immediately, Agent Perin."

Perin got to his feet. "Yes, sir, General."

Perin stalked out of the office, impelled by his serious purpose. Abello got on the phone immediately.

Crespin answered.

"You won't believe the stroke of luck we have just had," Abello said.

ARMY GENERAL Ramon Valcarce started awake in his bed. The ceiling of his bedroom was awash in red and blue lights, as if a spacecraft were landing on the lawn. He rolled out of bed in a hurry.

His wife sat up. "What is it?"

"I don't know."

Valcarce dragged on a robe and was tying it as he descended to the first floor of the house, a large four-bedroom structure in a neighborhood in the north end of Havana populated almost exclusively by upper-echelon government officials.

As he reached the bottom of the stairs his front door burst open and four military police charged inside, armed with AK-47s.

Valcarce stopped at the bottom stair and watched them silently.

A man in plainclothes entered behind the police, and on the

lawn were at least a dozen other soldiers. Valcarce struggled to place the man's face.

"Who are you?"

The plainclothesman withdrew a badge billfold and displayed it briefly. "Joel Perin, military Intelligence," he said. "You are under arrest, General. Please come with me."

"What am I being arrested for, Agent Perin?"

"Conspiring to overthrow the government of the People's Republic of Cuba."

"You must be joking!"

"I am not joking, General. I am operating under the authority of the president. Please come along peacefully."

The general nodded. "All right. Let's go."

There was a government car waiting and police and military vehicles parked at the curb, with at least a dozen other similar vehicles up and down the street. Valcarce allowed himself to be guided into the back of the government car and found, waiting inside, his longtime friend and comrade General Oswaldo Solana.

"Sol, what the hell is going on here?"

Solana shrugged. "I was hoping you knew."

COLONEL MATERA LOOKED at the orders in his hands and shook his head.

"I don't understand this at all."

"You're not supposed to," Crespin said. "You're simply supposed to obey."

"If there is danger within Cuba, why move troops away from the island?"

"There is no danger within Cuba. The danger comes from without. You will understand the purpose of these orders if the danger arises. If the danger does not arise, then you will simply have gone on an extended exercise and no harm will be done."

"But what good could possibly come from moving so many ships to such distant, isolated coordinates?"

"Enough, Colonel! I will not have these orders questioned further!"

Crespin got to his feet and paced back and forth behind his desk. "You've heard about the trouble. You know there have been many arrests tonight. There has been a serious compromise to the security of this nation. At this time we need orders followed to the letter. We do not need hotheaded colonels second-guessing the president's strategy! Do you understand?"

"Yes, General."

"Now I want those orders carried out, immediately and as specified. If you feel you are incapable of carrying out these orders, then tell me now and I will assign someone else to the command of these ships."

Matera rose to his feet, face reddening. It had been years since he had been rebuked like an errant corporal. "That will not be necessary, General."

"Good." Crespin glanced at his watch and sat at his desk again. "I expect you to be under way by midnight. Dismissed."

Matera strode out in a hurry.

GENERAL ABELLO MARCHED into the briefing room and brought instant quiet.

He spoke swiftly. "I know there has been a lot of speculation about what has occurred in the past several hours. I can only confirm for you that this agency, acting under the authority of the president and vice president themselves, this evening arrested several high-ranking officials in all branches of the military. We have very good reason to believe that most or all of these officials are members of a conspiracy to overthrow the government of the People's Republic of Cuba—or at least to remove the president and vice president from power."

He allowed the men to mutter among themselves for several seconds, then cleared his throat for silence. "What I am about to tell you is to be considered highly confidential and shall not be discussed outside this room with anyone, including among yourselves. Is that understood?"

There were nods throughout the room. "We are expecting the first attack to come tomorrow morning at dawn, at the National Assembly."

"Why the National Assembly?" one of the agents asked.

"The rebels know we are on to them. They know that under no circumstances will we permit the president and vice president to be at their homes at the Palace of the Revolution tomorrow morning as they would usually be. The palace, of course, was the original target. The rebels know that with our discovery of their intentions there is no chance they will be able to get at the president and vice president or their families at all. They'll target the National Assembly instead. Therefore, we are repositioning all agents to the National Assembly, except for a small, skeletal contingent."

Another agent stood. "General, if the rebels know we are on to them, and if they know that so many of their allies in the Cuban military have been arrested, why are we assuming they will still attack tomorrow at all? Wouldn't they wait to regroup?"

"No," Abello stated. "They will strike as soon as possible, before we uncover the full breadth of their plans, before we can prepare ourselves adequately. The longer they wait, the better our chances of discovering the full scope of their plans and erecting shields against their offenses. Questioning of the prisoners is proceeding now. Hopefully we'll know more by dawn and will be better prepared to respond." Abello sighed. He looked weary. "I don't have to tell you that this may be the most dangerous hour for our president and his revolution. We must be prepared to fight for him. We must be prepared to defend his ideals with our lives, if necessary."

He stood silent for a moment and allowed the weight of his words to settle on the men.

"Dismissed."

Perin sat at the rear of the room, watching the agents file out. When the room was empty he looked over the rows of chairs at General Abello, contemplative.

"You've done good work tonight, Joel," Abello said.

"Have I?"

"What do you mean by that?"

"Have I done good work or have I done *your* work?"

Abello leaned on his podium and clasped his hands in front of him, a study in calm patience. "You see a difference?"

"You're a part of the rebels' scheme, aren't you?"

"Is that what you think?"

Perin sat forward, leaning his elbows on his knees. "Yes. Now I do."

Abello nodded. "Well, you're right. I am. What tipped you off?"

"Nothing specific. Instinct, I suppose."

"You're a good agent."

"I thought so, before now. But I've arrested innocent men this evening, haven't I?"

"Innocent? No. But the men you arrested tonight were not a part of our New Revolution. General Serra implicated them—a very intelligent move on his part. We could not have engineered it better. Now our most powerful enemies are behind bars."

"What about these men?" Perin asked, making a gesture that included the entire meeting room. "You've sent them on a fool's errand, haven't you?"

Abello couldn't help but smile. "Right. Their ordered silence will insure that no one ever makes the connection that the president and vice president should be out of the palace. The palace is going to be virtually empty of guards when our Russian friends strike."

"Russian?"

"Yes, Joel. Ex-KGB, mostly. With their help we're going to recreate Cuba in Castro's original vision. We'll transform it into a pure Marxist-Leninist nation, removing it from the shackles of Castro's failed economy. Cuba will change from a slowly strangling nation to the model of success that will motivate a series of new Communist revolutions. The twenty-first Century will be the Century of Hope that the twentieth might have been, had not the dictators and the zealots betrayed the Marxist vision.''

Perin smirked humorlessly. ''Listen to yourself. You sound like you're reading cheap propaganda.''

''I am describing a pure vision of the future, Joel, a future that will be upon us in just a few hours. Our army is going to be striking at a virtually undefended palace before the sun rises. By dawn the president will be dead and a postmortem trial will be conducted in the People's Supreme Court, guarded by our army, of course. The president and his brother will be found guilty of betraying the people of Cuba through their own capitalist leanings. It will be proved that they have essentially stolen from the government—a death penalty under their own law. The People's Court and the rest of the government will be forced to either turn against them or face the death punishment with them. By noon tomorrow it will be announced that Cuba's judicial body, hearing evidence provided by Cuba's own ministry heads, has found the president and vice president guilty and approved their execution, and a new, orthodox Communist government will take control.''

''You expect the rest of Cuba to go along with this lunacy?''

Abello smiled and stood straight, arranging his papers. ''Yes, I do. Because our actions will not be perceived as lunacy, not by the Communist Party of Cuba. Not once we are in power.''

Perin considered it all carefully. He stood. ''It just might work, General. But I'm not going to let it.''

''I'm afraid you won't have much choice.''

Perin shrugged and made for the door. ''You'll have to shoot me in the back, General.''

''So be it, Joel.''

The sound of the .45-caliber gunshot filled the room. Perin flew into the closed door and collapsed on the floor.

Two agents flung open the door and stared down in shock at the dead man.

Abello withdrew the handgun from behind the podium and

tucked it into the holster under his jacket. He glanced at the massive hole that had been created in the front of the podium and shook his head.

"Can you believe he wanted to recruit me?" Abello asked quietly. "We won't tell his wife he was one of the traitors."

15

Straits of Florida, 24°N

"Striker? Where are you?"

"I'm back where I was dropped off, minus my four companions. They fell victim to the enemy."

"Damn it."

"I nearly bought it myself. But I managed to take out the Forger."

"I take it they're still in business?"

"Yeah. I was somewhat outnumbered, especially after I lost the SEALs."

"That's a tough pill to swallow—no matter how often I've had to take similar medicine."

"What can you tell me about activity to Cay Zucar?"

"You should be able to tell me that, shouldn't you? But I do have news," the big Fed said. "A plane departed the cay in the past hour and headed directly to Cuba. It seemed to get into the country without any security problems whatsoever. They must have confederates in air security who are insuring they're ignored."

"Where exactly are they going?"

"An airfield just west of the city of Cárdenas, which means they're within a short drive of Havana. I'd guess that airfield is going to serve as one of the staging grounds."

"Then that's where I'm headed," Bolan said.

"What's the plan?"

"I won't know until I get there. I'll have to recruit some Cubans."

"That might be tough. The Cuban military forces are mobilizing, which is keeping plenty of people in Washington awake tonight."

"Mobilizing against whom?" Bolan asked.

"That seems to be a big question, even to the Cubans. They're moving all sorts of men and equipment, but it's all going away from Havana and away from the island itself. There's no single geographic target, that's for sure. I'll bet that even the military heads don't know what the other military heads are up to. They're all operating under somebody else's orders, more or less. Either that or they're tied into the conspiracy and they're doing their best to get Cuba's military strength as far away from Cuba as possible. At this rate there won't be a soldier or a rifle left in Havana by morning."

"Which is when the strike takes place," Bolan said. "What's the chance of getting U.S. troops to help avert it?"

"Nil. We can't do anything that might be construed as helping Castro, first of all. If Castro falls and the U.S. is on the scene in any shape or form, we'll be blamed for it. On the other hand, what can you possibly do on your own?"

"I guess I'll see when I get there."

"Maybe you ought to let the Cubans handle this one themselves, Striker."

"The U.S. doesn't need radical, nuclear-capable Communist neighbors," Bolan said.

"We need you, however," Brognola offered.

"I'm going in, Stony Base."

Brognola sighed, his exasperation potent even over the radio speaker. Bolan had patched through using the satellite dish, which was still operating on the cay, where it had to have escaped detection. "Think we could go in by air?"

Bolan considered this. Flying aircraft over Havana would normally be next to impossible. However, the Russians had to be attempting a large-scale shutdown of Cuba's strategic air defense systems. How else did they plan on inserting their own soldiers? "Yeah," he said. "Maybe."

"All right. Grimaldi's taking off in a chopper now. He'll get you as close as possible to Havana. We'll go in at low altitude and see how close we can get before the Cubans send an MiG up our ass."

"And what if the Cubans have enough of their defense system operating to ID us?"

"We'll have to lie through our teeth. Say we had navigational problems or some such bullshit."

"Fine with me if you want to risk taking the heat," Bolan said. "I'm approximately two miles east of the cay now."

"Right. Proceed due south for twenty-five miles and watch for our pilot friend."

They said their goodbyes, then Bolan flipped off the radio and started the boat.

The Soviet gunboat was fully fueled and prepped for the quick trip to Cuba. Bolan took it to top speed, ripping through the Caribbean waters. The wind whistled in his ears and was cold against his skin.

He was wearing camou pants. He had left the shoes and socks in the ocean when he'd begun his swim. He hoped Grimaldi was bringing some extra clothes.

He put down anchor and waited at the meeting spot. He was there less than an hour before he heard the rumble of engines and watched the illuminated parade of Russian seacraft proceeding to their meeting point at Cárdenas.

Bolan's stolen gunboat sat dark and silent, and they never saw him.

THE BELL JetRanger threw up clouds of ocean mist as it descended like a gigantic drone, filling the night with its buzz. Bolan grabbed at the rope ladder and clambered inside the helicopter. Grimaldi gave him a quick wave as Bolan pulled in the ladder and slammed the door shut behind him.

"This time you aren't going in without me, Striker."

The Executioner clapped his old friend on the shoulder. "I'm glad to hear it."

Grimaldi laid on the stick, and the JetRanger climbed at a steep angle, headed directly south.

"What I don't understand is what we're going to do once we get there."

Bolan shrugged. "Stop a national revolution."

Grimaldi grinned. "Yeah. Okay."

San Miguel del Padrón, Cuba

AIR DEFENSE FORCE Colonel Hannah had been keeping an eye on the radar operator for over an hour, although the operator didn't know it. When he saw the man suddenly cock his head, the colonel knew the moment had come, and stalked up behind him.

The operator heard him and turned briefly. "Colonel, I was just going to call you. Look at this." He indicated the radar screen, where an alarming mélange of blips had appeared suddenly.

"What do you make of it, Colonel?"

"I make nothing of it and neither shall you, Corporal."

"Sir?"

"You are to ignore those indicators, do you understand?"

"But, Colonel—"

"You are not to discuss this with myself or anyone else. You are to alert no one else in this facility to the presence of those incoming vessels."

The operator was mystified. "That's entirely against security procedure."

"These are my orders."

The operator stared at the screen again, filled with doubt, watching the incoming vessels. The colonel still sensed resistance. He bent and spoke in a low voice so that the other night-shift staff couldn't hear.

"I am not going to explain this to you, Corporal, but these

are my orders and if they are not obeyed you will be arrested for violating national security, do you understand?''

The corporal acquiesced. "Yes, sir."

The colonel walked away, but he sat at his desk and kept an eye on the operator.

The operator sat and watched the incoming blips, helpless.

Cárdenas, Cuba

AIR DEFENSE FORCE Colonel Ruiz entered the briefing room quickly and, with a nod, had his assistant shut the door behind him. A scan of the seats revealed three men he knew to be loyal to the New Revolution and five men he judged to be willing to join the New Revolution once it began. The next few hours would tell.

"You all know what has occurred in Havana tonight," he said. "A large number of traitors and suspected traitors have been arrested. There may be more arrests in the next few hours."

There were a few cold faces, a few worried faces and one man, Major Guanare, had the aspect of no longer trusting anyone around him.

"We have been put on high-priority alert. Investigative forces will be moving into Cárdenas within the hour, including teams supplied by our friends in Russia."

Guanare spoke up. "Excuse me, sir, why are we bringing in the Russians? They should not be involved in matters of Cuban national security."

"The Russians helped us put together our system of national security. In fact they were far more involved than many of us know. They know what our strengths and weaknesses are, and they can help us evaluate our current situation."

"They're no longer our brethren, and I don't trust them, to be frank, sir."

"It will help ease your worries, Major, to know that the

men coming to our aid are former KGB representatives, not new-age Russians."

"That's worse, in my opinion," Major Alexandros put in. "The KGB has no business getting involved in our affairs. They're an obsolete organization, and they've been dismantled with good reason."

"The KGB helped us for years to weed out our ranks," Guanare said flatly.

"Our ranks no longer need to be culled of the type of people the KGB found intolerable. We need people with new ideas and unorthodox opinions to drive our national future."

"We need to arrest those people and trod them underfoot," Guanare stated.

"I'm firmly against allowing these dinosaurs into our midst, and I want to go on record as saying so," Alexandros said with a wave of his hand.

"So be it," Ruiz stated. "Regardless of your opinions, Major, the president himself has arranged for these men to assist us in our current crisis. They are arriving within the hour and they will arrive here, at Cárdenas. We will welcome them and cooperate with them in every way we can. Those are my orders and those are the orders of the president. Is that understood?"

Ruiz looked pointedly at Alexandros, who nodded and murmured his assent, as did every other person in the room.

"The most important assistance we can offer these men right now is noninterference. We are not to communicate with anyone outside this facility. This is also an order. Understood?"

Alexandros nodded.

"There will be more orders to come and I will convey them to you as soon as I learn them," Ruiz stated. "For now— dismissed."

Major Pitre stayed behind as the rest of the men filed from the briefing room. When he was alone with Colonel Ruiz he said, "Alexandros is too suspicious."

"Yes, he is. But Major Guanare is ready to join us."

"You think so? He is a volatile man. I find him difficult to read."

"He's ready," Ruiz declared. "Go talk to him. Let him know the score and see how he reacts."

"If he wants to join us?"

"Have him come to me."

"If he refuses to join the New Revolution?"

"Shoot him dead."

MAJOR RAUL ALEXANDROS watched the stream of boats that poured into the wharf at Cárdenas, his heart heavy, his mind so full of misgiving he could hardly contain it all.

There was definitely a crisis in Cuba, but he didn't believe it was what Colonel Ruiz said it was. There was far too much secrecy, far too much clandestine activity. Far too many high-ranking men in the Air Defense Force were being told to sit on their hands.

During the decade that he had been a DAAFAR major he had never been so out of touch with central command. He didn't know what was happening, and he didn't know why he was isolated. He didn't trust any of the reasons he had been given.

Alexandros strolled among the buildings and stood in the darkness watching the unloading proceedings. The men who poured off the crafts were speaking Russian and English. In fact a whole group of men was speaking English with distinctly American accents. Why would Americans be involved?

Others were speaking Spanish, but with Central American accents.

Why would Central Americans be involved?

None of it was right.

Alexandros had to get in touch with someone in central command and find out what was really going on. Turning sharply, he almost collided with Major Guanare.

"Major," Guanare said. "I am surprised to see you here."

"Why is that, Major?"

"You heard the colonel. We're to give the Russians their space."

"I did not know that meant I was confined to my quarters, Major."

They stared at each other in the icy darkness, and suddenly Alexandros was tired of playing elusive games. "You are a part of this conspiracy, aren't you, Guanare?"

Guanare lifted his hand as if in a shrug, but he leveled an automatic pistol at Alexandros in the darkness. "As of ten minutes ago I am, Alexandros."

He fired one time from a proximity of inches.

16

Straits of Florida, 23°N

The Bell 206B JetRanger II was a five-seater with an Allison C20 turboshaft engine generating 420-shp. It had an effective range of nearly five hundred miles, enabled by custom-fitted auxiliary fuel tanks.

"There's Cárdenas," Bolan said, spotting the first glimmer of light on the horizon.

"We have any clue where the Russians were headed—more specific than just 'Cárdenas'?" Grimaldi asked.

"I'd guess the navy docks."

Grimaldi gave him a look. "That'd be pretty ballsy, don't you think?"

"There's no way they're getting anywhere near the Cuban shore without getting picked up by radar. They've got to have people watching for them and downplaying their arrival. Maybe they've got so many people in their pockets they don't need to hide themselves. But those people are most likely in the military, which means they'll use the Revolutionary Navy wharf." He pulled out one of the detailed CIA maps of the island and scanned it quickly. "We ought to head directly into the wharf ourselves."

"Us they're not expecting. I don't see us getting the okay to set down right in the middle of it all."

"Of course not. But we'll still be showing up on their radar. If we head directly in without trying to hide then whoever is on watch may think we're part of the contingent."

San Miguel del Padrón, Cuba

THE RADAR OPERATOR spotted another blip on his screen, caught in the widespread north-shore radar net put in place by DAAFAR, the Cuban air force.

He looked around the room. Colonel Hannah was at his desk filling in a daily report, but stopped when he felt the operator's eyes on him.

The sound of quiet conversation came from two of the other operators on the far side of the room.

The corporal wondered what kind of orders they had received. He couldn't be the only one spotting all the strange vessels arriving that evening.

If everybody else had been given the same orders, then it had to be right. The words he was going to say to the colonel died in his throat. He turned back to his screen.

The blip was a little closer, coming directly into Cárdenas on the heels of the first wave. Maybe a straggler. Whoever it was, the operator chose not to see it.

Cárdenas, Cuba

THE RADAR OPERATOR grabbed the phone.

"Get me the colonel."

He waited, watching his screen. The blip was homing in directly on the wharf and the operator grew doubtful. Maybe he shouldn't even be bothering the colonel with this report.

But they had told him to expect a single group of vessels to arrive all at once at the dock and the single aircraft, which had landed at the nearby airfield. This little aircraft was slow-moving. Probably a chopper.

He heard the sounds of different voices on the other end of the phone trying to find the colonel.

Hell, it was coming directly at the wharf. It couldn't possibly be an unfriendly.

"We can't locate the colonel at the moment," somebody reported.

"Don't worry about it," the radar operator said.

He hung up.

BOLAN HAD FINISHED changing into the dry blacksuit Grimaldi had supplied. His face was streaked with dark combat cosmetics, and he had armed himself to the teeth.

The well-lit navy docks at Cárdenas were empty except for one area filled with intense activity. The Russian gunboats were there, and on the wharves a couple of Resnikoff's soldiers were herding the Colombians into a long line of cars and four-wheel-drive vehicles for the quick run to Cuba.

"Where's the airfield from here?"

"Two o'clock, about a mile off. Should be behind those barracks," Bolan said, indicating a group of low, illuminated buildings. Grimaldi steered the aircraft over the barracks, and they spotted another area of well-lit activity—and the parked Russian tactical transport aircraft.

"Put me down here," Bolan said.

"In the middle of their base?"

"No problem. Any real soldiers still stationed here will have been ordered to hole up. That way they can't interfere with the goings-on."

"How do you know that?"

"I don't, but it's a good working theory," Bolan replied.

Grimaldi reduced the rotor speed and the JetRanger descended slowly, braking to a halt and coming to a sudden hover at an altitude of about one yard.

Bolan hauled open the door and jumped to the ground.

"Testing," he said into the radio unit he had strapped to his head.

"I read you, Striker," Grimaldi said from inside the chopper.

"Meet you back here in ten minutes," Bolan said, and shot off into the darkness without giving the chopper a backward glance.

BOLAN SPOTTED FACES in the barracks windows, gazing at him with curiosity and frank suspicion, but without alarm or sense of immediacy, and he began to believe his own theory about the Cuban soldiers being locked inside. He jogged among the buildings and pulled himself to a quick halt in a shadowy spot at the end of one of the barracks that looked out over the docks. A group of four gunmen stormed up the incline from the docks, each armed with an AK-74.

They were coming to see who or what the helicopter was all about, but they didn't see Bolan lurking in the darkness. He dropped the long duffel bag he was carrying and waited, their excitement carrying them within a foot of him. His combat boot slammed into the first of the bunch, breaking his knee and sending him to the dirt, and he snatched the AK from the hands of the second gunman while he was still surprised. The assault rifle rattled in his hands, cutting a deadly swathe through the gunmen waist-high, chopping them down in a matter of seconds, then he directed the aim at the fallen man, taking him out of play before he could reach his weapon.

Bolan dropped the piece to the ground and unzipped the duffel in a long, sweeping motion. He withdrew an MM-1 multiround projectile launcher. The unit's exaggerated cylinder held twelve rounds, and Bolan had loaded it with alternating incendiary and HE rounds.

He stooped as his position started to take gunfire from the bottom of the hill, where the organized deployment of the Colombians into their vehicles had been transformed by the AK fire into a chaotic scramble.

He knelt, aimed with the forward pistol grip on the MM-1 and fired at the lead vehicle, which was making an attempt to put the buildings between itself and Bolan. The HE arced and hit the ground just a few feet from the four-wheel-drive vehicle, exploding and crushing the front end. It rolled into the grass on fire. A rear door opened, and a man jumped out screaming as the vehicle exploded in a ball of flame, throwing the burning man into the grass where he tumbled like a flaming log.

The second car had come to a screeching halt to avoid a similar fate, and Bolan sent the second round into its open window. There were screams of horror, then a huge belch as four tongues of white-orange flame licked the windows.

Bolan targeted all of the cars down the line until he was pushing the range of the projectile launcher. By then the rear line of cars and every visible man were turning tail and heading down the narrow asphalt wharf in the other direction.

He stopped and reloaded the MM-1, then took up one of the unfired AK-74s and grabbed the magazines from the other unfired weapons. With the Kalashnikov under one arm and the launcher under the other, he jogged down the hill.

He found no one alive among the infernos he had created, and at the road he trotted right. He spotted the line of cars and headed toward them at top speed. There had to be at least twenty more cars in the party train, several of them stopping to let the rest of the men on foot cram in.

Bolan aimed the launcher high and squeezed off several rounds, feeling the unit lose weight as one 40 mm explosive after another sailed high and crashed into the vehicles with devastating results. Every vehicle came to a burning halt—except for the few at the front that sought to distance themselves from the fires behind them. Bolan sent his last three HEs barreling straight into the windshields of the approaching vehicles, then dropped the empty MM-1 and aimed the AK-74 directly at the surviving drivers. There was a burst of gunfire from several of the cars and Bolan triggered at the sources of the fire, feeling the heat of their rounds whiz close by before he dived behind the nearest building and out of range. He dropped the emptied mag and rammed in another as the surviving front-line vehicles accelerated to get past him. He fired directly through the open passenger-side window of the first car.

He aimed at the second car but couldn't see the driver through the opaque, shattered windshield, so he simply triggered off the rest of his rounds at the approximate location of the steering wheel. The vehicle lurched suddenly to the left and spun to a halt at the side of the road, motionless.

The last car reached top highway speeds and flew by Bolan as the AK cycled dry. He fell to the ground to avoid a flurry of autofire from the rear window of the vehicle. It spun ninety degrees and accelerated up the incline into the barracks.

They'd be back. Meanwhile, Bolan changed his last AK mag and looked for more targets. The line of burning cars separated him from the rear group of vehicles, still twelve or thirteen strong. They were fleeing in the other direction, and he didn't waste bullets on them.

JUST BECAUSE the JetRanger wasn't rigged for combat didn't mean Grimaldi was helpless. He took the helicopter into the night sky in a smooth slow spiral that gave him an expanding view of the wharf, the barracks and the rest of the base, including the airfield just behind the barracks, containing the Antonov An-32 Russian tactical transport plane. He spotted the bulky shape heading down the runway at an idle pace and knew they had arrived on the scene with just minutes to spare. The An-32 was about to take off again, target Havana.

Not if Grimaldi had anything to do with it. He laid on the stick and swept the JetRanger toward the airfield. The Russian aircraft came to a forward halt and pivoted like a great whale in a large circle that brought it back to the runway, positioned for takeoff.

Grimaldi reached for the pack of grenades and put them on the seat next to him. He yanked open the large side door and spun the JetRanger into a swooping curve that tilted the world in his direction. He snatched up a grenade, thumbed the pin and let the lethal egg fall out the side of the helo, then grabbed another.

So far he spotted no ground crew, and he had no way of knowing if the pilot of the An-32 saw him. The first grenade exploded on the tarmac.

"WHAT THE HELL was that?" Colonel Resnikoff shouted, jumping out of his seat and storming into the cockpit, in time to witness another explosion just to the front of the plane.

"There's a helicopter up there grenading us!" the pilot shouted.

"We're also getting reports from Ruiz—the vehicles are being attacked," the radioman said.

"By whom?" Resnikoff demanded. "Get this plane in the air!" he shouted to the pilot.

"As fast as I can!"

There was another explosion, this one unseen, but it shook the aircraft.

"We're hit!" the radioman exclaimed.

"Not bad!" the pilot added. "We're still accelerating and all engines are functioning!"

The copilot chimed in. "Pressure drop in number-two engine."

Resnikoff slammed his fist into the wall. "Fuck!"

"We can still get off the ground," the pilot declared.

GRIMALDI ALMOST CHEERED when the grenade exploded near one of the plane's engines, but the prop slowed only slightly and the aircraft continued to increase speed. It was going to take off in seconds.

Grimaldi flooded fuel into the engines and rocketed into a high-speed horizontal acceleration, flying the gauges into the red. The stick shuddered in his grip and he craned his neck to see the runway, inching ahead of the An-32. He grabbed another grenade, thumbed the pin and tossed the bomb. He swore, convinced his accuracy was off and grabbed another explosive. One after the other, he sent down four more deadly eggs. The first hit in the grass to the right of the runway, then one-two-three the rest of them hit the asphalt and churned up the path of the oncoming transport plane.

THE COPILOT SHOUTED in terror when he saw the runway erupt, pitting craters in their direct path.

"Abort!" the copilot shouted.

"Get off the runway and accelerate!" Resnikoff ordered harshly.

"We'll never make it," the pilot declared.

"Get off the runway and get this plane in the air!" Resnikoff withdrew his Makarov handgun and aimed it at the pilot's head.

The pilot fed fuel to the huge Ivchenko AI-20M engines, which increased their pitch and propelled the plane onto the grassy earth. The An-32 shook violently, and Resnikoff was nearly knocked off his feet as the wheels plowed through the field. The pilot leaned on the controls and the roar of the props became throaty whines of exertion, then the wheels left the ground, hit it again with a bounce and spun into empty air.

GRIMALDI WRENCHED the controls, and the JetRanger tried to respond to the change in direction. At last it swept after the fleeing Russian aircraft, too little too late. The An-32 seemed to leap into the air, crash back down again, then suddenly become airborne. It labored tremendously for every narrow foot of altitude it gained, and the JetRanger struggled valiantly to catch up. Then the huge prop plane got its second wind and rose into the sky, leaving the JetRanger farther and farther behind.

17

Matanzas, Cuba

The JetRanger leveled off over the city of Matanzas, a dark mass of buildings in the night that resembled one of the sprawling shantytowns that circled Mexico City like a growing cancer. This was one of Cuba's largest metropolises and, like all Cuban cities, it suffered power outages almost daily.

The only real lights were on the roads, where a few random cars came and went here and there. There was little purpose for Matanzas's civilians to be out in the night.

At an altitude of two thousand feet the caravan of cars on the highway was impossible to miss.

"There they are," Bolan said when it was still nothing but a collection of fast-moving specks in the distance.

"Let's move in."

"Wait," Bolan said, tapping the CIA map in his hands. "This shows a bridge ahead over a section of bay just outside the city."

"Yeah?"

"That might give us a decent opportunity to incapacitate the entire caravan at one time. I'm thinking of something a little more precise than egging them from the skies with hand grenades."

"I get the picture," Grimaldi said as he accelerated the JetRanger.

"Think we have time to get in and get out before they reach it?"

Grimaldi grimaced, still smarting from the escape of the An-32. "I'll make the time."

Bolan rummaged in the equipment pack and withdrew the detonators and C-4.

"There. Put down at the far end."

Bolan opened the door to the JetRanger and jumped out before the craft could settle on the pavement. The bridge was old and cracked, and the railing was made of poured concrete with decorative triangular gaps—an adequate hiding place. Bolan would have preferred a more central point to plant the C-4. It was so close to one edge he doubted the explosion would down the entire width of the bridge.

Time was short. He ran to the railing, activated the detonator, stuffed the package into the hiding place and bolted back to the JetRanger, diving for the seat.

"Get out of here. They'll be here any minute."

The rotor pitch increased suddenly and the helo bolted ahead at an altitude of less than ten feet, then veered up and out, away from the bridge and away from the encroaching caravan. They increased altitude and scanned for the caravan.

They couldn't find it.

"What would they stop for?" Grimaldi asked.

"Nothing," Bolan replied. "Maybe they're in hiding. Maybe they suspect a trap."

Grimaldi yanked on the stick, and the JetRanger leaned into a sharp turn to the south. If the caravan had headed off-road, it couldn't have gone far. They passed over darkened small towns and Havana suburbs. There was little illumination anywhere, just a few blinking radio towers, powered by generators.

And then they saw a flash of red. Bolan leaned out the door of the JetRanger to see it more clearly. It was a single car running without headlights. Its brake lights had come on momentarily, but when they were off the car faded in the glare from the JetRanger's running lights.

"Can you run this thing dark?"

"Yeah." Grimaldi flipped some switches and the JetRanger

became utterly black, like a great invisible noisy bug fluttering in the night sky.

Bolan stared down. It took a moment for the ghosts of the light to fade from his vision, then he spotted them—a long line of vehicles running dark on the highway. As if to confirm their discovery, another car's red brake lights flared briefly and were gone.

"The caravan is almost directly below us," he told his pilot.

"They thought they could sneak around us."

"Well, they still have to get back on the highway if they want to get to Havana anytime soon. Meanwhile we have to go back and get that plastique."

"What a waste of time!"

"You can't expect every trick to work every time," Bolan said, "and we can't go leaving high explosives lying around for innocent Cubans to stumble across tomorrow morning."

"NOW WHAT ARE they up to?" Quinones demanded.

"You've got me," his driver said, leaning forward to stare up through the windshield. "I'm sure they spotted us."

But the helicopter was veering away and to the east, back the way it had come.

"They're probably running low on fuel or explosives or both," suggested the gunman in the seat with Quinones, Perez, one of his most trusted guards.

Quinones watched the dark aircraft fade into the unlit night sky. "Maybe. Or they are going to bring reinforcements."

"From where?" the driver asked. "I thought we were supposed to have clear sailing all the way."

"That's what I was told," Quinones declared. "But they've had somebody on their ass every step of the way. The guy that took out their mercs in Guatemala. A CIA agent or somebody."

"CIA?" Perez queried. "No way, Manny. Those guys aren't too good working independently, you know? They need to have lots of support. If they've got a single guy on their ass, he's got to be Special Forces or something."

Quinones watched the black night sky. The helicopter was no longer visible, but he felt the menacing shadow of its presence. "Or something." He grabbed the radio and broadcast over the band the rest of the cars were tuned into. "We're heading back to the highway, and we're going to eat some miles and try to make up lost time."

THE JETRANGER SPENT even less time sitting on the bridge than its first stop. Bolan bolted to the crevice and snatched his package of high explosives and was sitting in the passenger seat again in fifteen seconds. They were off the ground before he'd even bothered to deactivate the detonator. The tiny red glow of the LED faded.

Once again they were airborne and hunting for the caravan of vehicles. They found it as it was pulling onto the highway again, still running black. But with the other traffic on the highway it was too dangerous for the caravan to continue without lights, and the thirteen automobiles and sport-utility vehicles lit up like a Christmas tree in a city square.

Grimaldi was flying well behind the caravan.

"Any other likely traps?" he asked.

Bolan dropped the laminated map. "No. Let's just get in there and see what kind of damage we can do."

The Stony Man pilot fed the rotors thrust and the bird picked up speed and altitude rapidly until they were again hovering a thousand feet above the caravan.

"Think they've noticed us?" Grimaldi asked.

The front car began to swerve and weave suddenly, and a head poked out the rear window.

"Yeah," Bolan said. "Get us down there."

The JetRanger tilted and plummeted, and Bolan yanked the pin from an HE grenade and held the bomb out the open side of the aircraft. He released it; for a moment the grenade moved gently away from the helicopter, its descent speed minimalized by the descent of the helicopter, giving it the appearance of slow motion. Then he saw it home in on the lead car, and the face in the rear window disappeared suddenly. The car swerved to the left and the grenade hit the pavement. The second car drove into the bright explosion and the front end sailed off the ground, the tires vaporized and the engine transformed into flying scrap metal. The car crashed to the ground again and rolled onto its side.

As the first car screeched to a halt, the Executioner grabbed another HE grenade, arming it and flinging it at the stopped car as the passengers exited. The driver froze and stared at the plummeting bomb, but the passengers in the rear jumped for cover. The driver lurched into action just before the grenade hit, but it was too little too late. The explosion snuffed him out in a blast that burned off his flesh. The front end of the car was crushed as if it had been in a crash with an invisible train.

One of the rear passengers screamed on the ground, the skin and much of the flesh that had been his back and legs flayed and burned away. The other passenger jumped to his feet, apparently unharmed, and aimed a handgun at the JetRanger.

But Grimaldi rotated the helo and hit the gas, propelling the chopper along the length of the caravan as it came unsteadily to a halt. Bolan tossed three more grenades and felt the satisfying rumble of the detonations in the helo's wake.

The JetRanger elevated and spun 180 degrees, swinging the ruin of the caravan back into view. The passenger from the first car was unloading his handgun in their direction, although the helo was now well out of range. His bullets would have been better spent issuing a mercy round to his comrade, convulsing just a few steps away. Two more cars were engulfed in flame, and a fuel tank exploded with a flash.

"Good work," Grimaldi commented.

"Not good enough. They're going to make a break for it."

The man with the handgun sprinted to the nearest undamaged 4WD vehicle, stepped into the front passenger side of the vehicle and shouted back to the other cars.

Bolan grabbed his field glasses and peered through them at the shouting man.

"Friend of yours?" Grimaldi asked.

"Manuel Quinones."

"Ha! There's nothing I like better than putting drug scum out of business." He leaned forward in his seat like an enthusiastic video-gamer and steered the JetRanger into the pull of gravity, swooping down at the shouting figure. Quinones's face was a study in terror as he spotted the attacking helicopter.

"I'll give you target in three, two, one!" Grimaldi shouted, and twisted the diving aircraft violently, presenting the sport-utility vehicle to Bolan, who had snatched at the reloaded MM-1 and triggered it twice in rapid succession, sending twin HE 40 mm projectiles rocketing at the vehicle. Grimaldi twisted the JetRanger at the final second to keep from clipping the car, and the projectiles skimmed the top and hit the ground ten feet from the vehicle. They blasted one after another, and the sudden inferno wafted toward the chopper, assisting the screaming rotors.

"Damn. Sorry!" Grimaldi said. "Now they're taking off!"

"They're still fish in a barrel," Bolan growled. "Get us overhead."

San Miguel del Padrón

"RESNIKOFF! COME IN!"

"What's happening?"

"We're getting the shit blown out of us, that's what!"

"Where are you?"

"We're just entering some town called San Miguel..."

"What? You're way behind schedule!"

"There's not going to be *any* of us left to keep your damned schedule if we don't get some help! We're down to nine vehicles already!"

Quinones heard the general utter a Russian expletive. "The bastard in the helicopter?"

"Who do you think!"

"Why haven't you taken him out?"

"With what? Listen, Resnikoff, you better get us some assistance and you'd better get it for us right now, or we're turning around and going back the way we came!"

Over Havana

RESNIKOFF SLAMMED DOWN the receiver on the radio of the Russian aircraft and swore again.

"Get me General Vincent," he said to the radio operator. The operator spun his dials and, speaking Spanish, raised a ground operator at the air command base. "Code Red Hammer for General Vincent."

Resnikoff grabbed the receiver. "Vincent?"

"Vincent here."

"Resnikoff. We've got an emergency."

"You should be at T minus eleven minutes."

"We have a delay! There's some American joker in a helicopter taking out our ground-based forces with explosives!"

The general considered this. "What do you want me to do about it?"

"Get us some air assistance."

"You know the plan, Resnikoff. We go into action once the deed is done, not before."

"The deed's not going to get done if we don't have ground support, and our ground support is getting exterminated as we speak."

"All right. I'll see what I can do," the general said hesitantly. "I'll get you something."

Resnikoff spit out the coordinates of the auto caravan and threw down the receiver.

San Miguel del Padrón

"HANNAH, THIS IS Vincent."

"Yes, General Vincent?" Hannah unconsciously sat up straighter in his seat as he spoke into the phone.

"There's trouble and we need to supply some assistance." Vincent briefly told Hannah the situation and fed him the coordinates. "Get an attack chopper up there to divert the attacks."

"How am I supposed to do that, General?"

"I don't know, but all our plans are riding on success tonight. And success is not going to come about without some air assistance from us *now*. Get a Hind up and do it quietly."

"You want me to send an assault helicopter on a combat mission and you want it done without anybody knowing?" Hannah asked incredulously.

"That's exactly what I want. Do it now."

Hannah couldn't argue further because the general had hung up.

The colonel raced down a narrow corridor to a nearby barracks and quickly found the man he was looking for.

"Captain Juan," he said quietly, giving the sleeping man a shove. "Juan!"

The man stirred and sat up suddenly. He squinted in the dim light. "Colonel Hannah?"

"Shh. Get up. Quick and quiet. This is an emergency."

Juan dressed and met the colonel in the hallway three minutes later.

"These are my orders. Get up in an Mi-24 as fast as you can. A group of automobiles is being attacked by an American helicopter at these coordinates. You are to go and waste the American chopper. You are to ask no questions and you are to tell no one. Understand?"

Captain Emilio Juan looked at the piece of paper for a full five seconds. "I understand," he said hesitantly.

"Then get moving."

THE LINE OF CARS suddenly started to slow. In seconds they had drawn ranks on the highway and had begun to get out and lay their automatic weapons over the roofs of the vehicles.

"They're making a stand," Bolan said.

"No problem," Grimaldi answered. "We'll simply get di-

rectly above them, high enough to be out of range. Then w
drop grenades on them.''

Bolan shook his head. "I've got a feeling they've got re
inforcements coming.''

"Airborne reinforcements?"

"If they've got pull with the military, it stands to reason.'

"We're no match for a combat chopper," Grimaldi said.

"I know it.''

"We've got two choices. One, stay and get shot out of th
sky or two, get the hell out of here. What'll it be?''

Bolan scanned the horizon. "Three—set an ambush. I'd be
my paycheck those guys aren't in direct contact with th
DAAFAR so they won't be able to warn the chopper off.''

"I'd agree with that. Who signs your paycheck, anyway?'
Bolan ignored the question.

"What if they send two choppers?" Grimaldi asked.

"We're SOL. But I'm guessing that the Cubans are tryin
to keep their involvement to a minimum at this stage. We'
hope for one.''

"Okay, what's the strategy?"

CAPTAIN EMILIO JUAN didn't like this at all. One man alon
in a chopper, sent up by a colonel without regard for regula
protocol. What kind of an assignment was this, anyway? Wh
was there a hostile American helicopter roaming the outskirt
of Havana? Who was it after? Why wasn't the entire Cuba
strategic air command being called out to bring down th
chopper?

He was flying a Soviet-built Mil Mi-24D-Hind D gun
ship with a fifty-six-foot rotor diameter, powered by two
1,500-shp TV-2 turboshafts. The gunship was mounted with
57 mm rockets and 12.7 mm machine gun. It was designe
for operation by at least two men, a pilot and a gunner, bu
Captain Juan felt no disadvantage at being alone in the chop
per when his opponent was flying an unarmed civilian heli
copter. It allowed him to operate the gunship on his own terms
following his own rules, with no second-guessing. He enjoye

the sensation of flying and fighting in combination. His hands could move from control to control with speed and accuracy, and he could fire and fly with instinctive skill.

If every other aspect of this mission bothered him, he was looking forward to actual combat.

He was about to be terribly disappointed.

He reached the coordinates within minutes and circled the strange configuration of automobiles on the highway. There were maybe ten cars and thirty men, carrying automatic weapons, shotguns and handguns. A few even aimed their weapons at him as he approached before identifying him.

There was no American helicopter in sight.

He circled the caravan of cars as the men began to pour into them, and they started on their way together.

Captain Juan witnessed a flash of light off to the north—coming from the sea?

Several flashes followed and the regularity of the flashes convinced him he was seeing a warning light from an aircraft. That had to be his target. He activated his weapon systems and moved cautiously north across a stretch of overgrown land, to the burned-out hulk of an abandoned hotel that sat on a stretch of low cliff twenty feet above a wide, seaweed-strewed beach. Juan knew the building, knew it had been a popular tourist attraction prior to the coming of Castro and had stood there rotting for at least thirty years.

The Mi-24's searchlight scanned the beach and the wild growth of palm trees and weeds around the burned-out building. The emergency light from the other helicopter didn't repeat itself. Where the hell was it? It couldn't have just vanished. Had it fallen into the ocean?

A glimmer seemed to come from inside the rotting hulk of the hotel.

No—the chopper was hiding behind it, keeping the skeletal building between itself and the DAAFAR chopper. It was a commercial JetRanger, without any type of mounted weaponry.

A man leaned out the side of the JetRanger with what

looked like at first an oversize machine gun with a cylindrical
magazine. He was hidden behind a piece of the building, but
there was a flash of light and an explosion. Juan started. They
had no built-in weapon systems, but that guy had just fired a
grenade launcher!

But no handheld grenade launcher had range comparable to
what was mounted on the Mi-24. Juan need only get it out in
the open.

"HE'S GOT ALL KINDS OF bad stuff he can shoot at us. If we
get in his line of fire, we're dead," Grimaldi said needlessly.

Bolan didn't answer. He fired another high-explosive round
harmlessly into the ruin of the old ten-story building and
watched the Soviet-built combat chopper veer. Although the
explosion was entirely contained inside the building and
couldn't have touched the Cuban aircraft, the pilot was exer-
cising extra caution.

"Ready for our move?" Bolan asked.

"Yeah."

The Cuban pilot began to circle the building counterclock-
wise to give himself a clear shot.

"Now," Bolan said.

Grimaldi slammed the stick, and the JetRanger jumped forward clockwise and circled the building, bringing the Mi-24
into clear view. Bolan fired once, twice, three times, sending
40 mm HE grenades arcing in the direction of the aircraft. The
chopper stopped, swung in space and retreated backward
around the building to keep itself out of range of the grenades.

"He's getting there. Keep driving him," Bolan said.

The JetRanger tilted, and Bolan was forced to fire out and
up, careful to avoid hitting the JetRanger's rotors with his
grenades.

The Soviet chopper backed up farther.

"A little more."

"He's going to pull back from the building," Grimaldi
warned.

"Give me some more!" Bolan commanded.

Grimaldi wrenched on the control, and the JetRanger swerved dangerously close to the building, the erratic move forcing the Mi-24 to reverse itself ten more feet around the decrepit building.

"In position!" Grimaldi shouted.

Bolan slammed his fist into the red button on the radio transmitter. The red light died.

Directly above the Mi-24, tucked into the broken steel and concrete beams of the dead hotel, the C-4 exploded, taking a sudden chomping bite out of the corner of the hotel and raining massive bricks and chunks of rusted girders and pre-stressed concrete blocks to the ground. The rotors on the Mi-24 clanged and crashed against the storm of debris and the gunship plummeted at a stiff angle, hitting the beach with a crack of steel and glass and a whoosh of spilling fuel. The pilot tumbled out of the cockpit and jumped to his feet, racing down the beach; behind him the Soviet-built helicopter looked like a giant crushed mosquito, its twisted rotors, crippled and bent, lurching to a halt. There was a spark and the spilled fuel ignited.

Bolan saw the pilot put his hands on his hips and look up at the JetRanger.

"He's thanking his lucky socks he's alive, I guess," Grimaldi said, laughing.

"Yeah," Bolan growled. "Now let's go clean up some drug dealers."

18

The caravan was on the move again when the JetRanger found it a few miles farther down the highway. The Colombians were cruising at top speed, trying to make up lost time, and had probably assumed their nemesis was out of commission.

"We've got three grenades left. We need to make them count," Bolan said.

"We'll come up behind them and over them, just like before," Grimaldi replied.

He moved low to the ground and increased his speed until the JetRanger was coming up on the caravan. In its darkened state the gunmen in the vehicles knew it was there by the roar of the engines and the thunder of air around the rotors.

As Grimaldi raised the chopper to about twenty feet above the highway, Bolan dropped the first of the three grenades with surgical precision. It plummeted into the windshield of the second-last car. The HE detonated inside the sport utility vehicle, sending shrapnel and fire into the last car as well as the car in front of it. All three vehicles flew off the road into a low drainage ditch, the sound of the pileup matching the blast of the second grenade, which exploded between two cars. The car behind the pair crashed into them even before the force of the explosion had dissipated, and the three vehicles came to a rest in an fiery wreck.

But by then the vehicles at the front of the caravan had realized their predicament and were tearing away from the carnage. They quickly spaced themselves out.

"Who you want to go for?" Grimaldi asked.

"In front."

The JetRanger accelerated up and away from the freeway until it was hovering over the first of the four surviving vehicles. Grimaldi matched the speed of the car as it braked and accelerated in a vain attempt to shake the aircraft. The pilot's skill was such that to Bolan the car down below looked like it was sitting almost still under the helo while the world rushed around them.

He lobbed his last high explosive grenade and watched the bomb whirl to the distant pavement.

"WHO'S LEFT?" Quinones demanded.

"Jorge and myself," said one of the drivers over the radio.

"That's all—four cars?"

"That's it, Manny."

"What's it doing now?" Quinones shouted, leaning over the dashboard and watching the helicopter zip high above them. Then he knew. They were going to try to take out the front car.

"They're going after you, Car One," he shouted.

He dropped the mike and pushed himself out the passenger window, grabbing the top of the car and pulling out the AK-74 the Russians had given him. Then he saw the tiny flash of metal descending from underneath the chopper.

"Stop the car," he shouted and grabbed for the windowsill as the car slowed abruptly.

Car One stood up on its tail end like a trained dog, levitated by a pillow of yellow fire. Then the fire engulfed it and it fell onto its roof, crushing the front seat and sending jets of flame out the sides.

Manny Quinones hauled himself out the window and landed on his feet, slamming the AK onto the roof of his vehicle and firing at the helicopter. The chopper twisted to show Quinones its belly, and the 5.45 mm hollowpoint rounds rattled against the white surface, scarring the paint job.

The AK-74 chugged to a halt, and Quinones grabbed another magazine from his pocket, slamming it into place. But by the time he recommenced firing, the JetRanger was too high to score on.

He grabbed the mike through the window. "This is what we do—we separate and run dark. We meet at the palace gates as planned," he declared.

"Jesus, Manny, look what's happened to us," Perez said, from the back seat.

Quinones looked. Out of more than twenty cars, three remained. How many of his men had been killed in the past two hours?

His army was reduced to only a few loyal men—all for a cause he really didn't care about.

Perez was out of the car looking at him in the darkness of the highway.

"Let's go back, Manny. This isn't our fight! Let's get our guys that are still alive and get the hell out of this fucked-up country!"

Quinones looked at Perez, then up at the helicopter, which was hovering out of range as if it, too, was waiting for his decision. The chopper still ran dark, and he could see the dim shadows of two men in the bird. He tried to imagine their faces. What kind of men had the audacity to wipe out so many human beings so mercilessly?

He'd lost this fight. That was certain. But he would find out who was sitting in that helicopter if he had to use every contact he had in the United States. He'd track down those men and wipe them off the face of the earth if it took him the rest of his life to do it.

That determination was cold comfort at the moment.

"You're right. Let's go home." He grabbed the radio mike and spoke to the other two cars, parked not far away. "We're going home."

BOLAN GAZED through the field glasses. That was Manny Quinones. He was still alive and assessing his losses.

"No matter what Resnikoff's promised him, it can't be worth it at this stage," Grimaldi stated.

Bolan nodded. "I'm sure that's what he's thinking right now."

Then he saw the Colombian drug lord get back into his automobile. The three vehicles turned on the highway. Bolan noticed a distinct lack of urgency. They headed back the way they had come.

"They're out of our hair," Grimaldi said.

"Yeah." But Bolan was thinking that the name Manuel Quinones was still scrawled in his war book. He would face the drug lord again someday.

"You think the Russians will still attempt their strike without ground forces?" Grimaldi asked.

"Of course they will," Bolan said. "And they'll be more desperate than ever."

San Miguel del Padrón

"COLONEL HANNAH."

The colonel looked up from his nightly report. The man standing at his desk was DAAFAR General Miguel Barba.

He jumped to his feet, causing his chair to scoot back noisily. "General," he said, saluting smartly. The general had four armed military policemen accompanying him.

"Colonel Hannah, what's going on here?"

The colonel looked confused. Surely the general didn't know about the chopper....

"Your radioman alerted me to a report of a downed Mi-24," Barba said. "The pilot radioed that he was on a topsecret mission and was shot down."

The colonel said nothing as a waft of cold fear filled him.

"The radioman alerted me because he assumed I would be the one to know how to react, since it was a top-secret mission. The trouble is, I don't know anything about it."

"I don't know anything about it, either, General!" Hannah declared.

"The pilot claims you were the one who gave him the orders," Barba said. "I talked to him myself."

"No, General, it wasn't me."

"But the pilot is one of ours. Nobody else could have put up a chopper from this base tonight except you. You deny any knowledge of this?"

Hannah bowed his head, thinking furiously. "General, I was working under the direct orders of General Vincent."

"General Vincent doesn't have authority here, Colonel."

"I'm aware of that, sir. But he gave me orders anyway. He said they were top secret and authorized all the way to the top. He said I was not supposed to discuss this with anyone, which is why I didn't alert you, sir."

General Barba nodded quickly and said over his shoulder, "Get me Vincent."

Over Havana

"QUINONES HERE," said the radioman.

Resnikoff grabbed the mike. "Quinones, what's going on?"

"What's going on? I'll tell you what's going on. Your friends in the air force failed. We got the shit bombed out of us. You've got nothing left down here."

"What do you mean by that?"

"I mean that we have three cars left. Three cars, you asshole! Whoever is in that chopper has wiped out three-quarters of my men! No deal is worth those losses. You've ruined me, you power-crazy bastard!"

"What are you doing now?" Resnikoff demanded.

"Getting out of this godforsaken country and never coming back," Quinones declared. "I hope you rot in hell, Resnikoff."

The radioman in the Russian aircraft stared wide-eyed as Resnikoff kicked the wall repeatedly.

It took him a full fifteen seconds to stop, then he stood gazing blankly at the night sky over the dark capital of Cuba.

"We still have forty men in this aircraft," Resnikoff said to no one. His voice was thick, as if he were drunk, and his words spilled out too quickly, tripping over each other. "We have some of the hardest soldiers in the world and enough firepower to bring this city to its knees. All we have to do is get in and make our strike. There's no one there to stop us, and there's no one who even knows we're coming in. We still have more than enough firepower to make this work."

"You're still going in?" the pilot said.

"We're going in."

"You think we ought to tell Fagen we've lost our ground support?"

"No! I'll let them know myself when we're inside the palace."

The pilot wanted to say something else, but thought better of it. "We'll be in position in four minutes."

Resnikoff brought the mike to his lips again and the radio-man switched it to intercom. Resnikoff's voice filled the aircraft.

"Four minutes."

San Miguel del Padrón

"GENERAL VINCENT HAS denied any knowledge of your activities, Colonel Hannah."

Hannah put his head in his hands. "He knows. I swear he knows."

"I've worked with General Vincent for over two decades, Colonel," Barba said. "I trust him implicitly. You, however, I don't trust. I want to know why you sent that chopper out. Who was it attacking in the other helicopter? Why were you trying to maintain secrecy?"

Hannah said nothing. Vincent had himself set up nicely. There was nothing linking him to any of the covert activity. The colonel would be the one to take the fall. The more he tried to blame the general, the worse he would make it for himself.

"Hannah, if there is something going on tonight I want to know about it. If you start talking right now, I can guarantee you leniency."

Hannah looked up at Barba.

"If I find out about it too late, I can guarantee you will get the harshest punishment possible."

"What guarantee do I have of your sincerity?" Hannah asked.

"You have the word of a general."

Hannah almost laughed. He had trusted a general before and look at him.

What was even more ludicrous, even more ironic, he realized, was that he had no choice but to do so again.

He started to talk.

The National Assembly, Havana

THE DGA COLONEL LOOKED at the map of the National Assembly, now covered with green dots marking the troops he had deployed into the massive complex. In a few hours the representatives of the people of Cuba would begin to arrive for their daily activities. Soon the complex would be populated with thousands of human beings, the flesh of the Cuban national government. The strike would come then. He had to be ready for it. It might come from any entrance point, from the street, from the sky.

No matter where they came from, the attackers would meet with thronged resistance like they had never expected. The colonel's army and DGA forces blanketed the complex. Guards had been assembled from the military bases surrounding the city, and even from the palace itself.

The colonel was confident. But he studied the layout again and again. He had to be absolutely sure he had covered all his bases. He didn't want to leave a single weak spot in his strategy.

He would stop this so-called New Revolution before it even started.

Palace of the Revolution, Havana

HAVANA WAS EXPERIENCING one of its regular power outages. Even with full power, the city didn't give off the usual glow that could be seen for miles over other Western cities of similar size, a glow that would have illuminated the forty dark rectangular shapes that seemed to form in the middle of the night out of nothingness, birthed by the night sky itself. They descended over Havana in silence.

Antonio Colón, head of palace security, was standing nervously at his desk, looking over the electronic palace proximity maps. The palace was running on its generators, so he wasn't worried about losing his perimeter warning system. He was worried about his personnel problem.

A whole group of his men had been removed the week before for a training program recently instituted by one of the DGA generals. That had cut his staff by half. Then, earlier tonight, an emergency threat to the National Assembly had required more of his men to be siphoned off for temporary detail there. The staff on duty at the palace was less than skeletal. There was some kind of emergency, and yet the DGA had advised the president and the vice president to stay in the palace with their immediate families. It was something about a threat diverted from the palace to the National Assembly.

Colón evaluated guard positions on his electronic map. The palace hadn't been so scantily guarded when the president and the vice president and their families were in residence in all the years Colón had served on security detail. The palace had never been so vulnerable, almost as if someone had engineered it.

Such engineering would have required corruption at the

highest levels of national security, corruption Colón wouldn't have dreamed possible before tonight. But he had heard rumors of mass arrests among the highest echelons of the Cuban military.

The president and vice president had been meeting with their advisers for hours. Finally the meetings had broken up and the palace was growing quiet.

Colón would be glad when this night was over.

There was a shadowy movement on one of the fourteen black-and-white television monitors. Colón glanced at it, thinking it was one of the patrolling guards. Then he saw the collapsing shape of a parasail.

At that moment he knew that it was a setup.

The figure on the screen shrugged out of his harness and grabbed a shoulder-mounted projectile launcher of some type.

He aimed at a square utility building against the lower wall at one end of the palace, and the launcher flared with bright light.

Colón saw more shapes on the other monitors. More than he could count. Then he saw the launched projectile hit the low building and explode.

That was where the generator was, as well as the electrical mains for the backup generator. Somebody knew exactly what they were doing.

All the television monitors went black.

An emergency horn blared throughout the building, but an instant later even that went silent. Colón pulled out his belted walkie-talkie and spoke into it briefly.

"We have intruders. All entrances. Code red."

"Acknowledged," answered a voice from the radio. "Code red."

That would be good enough to get the president and vice president into their protective chamber, which was blast-proof. No matter how good these intruders were, they surely weren't good enough to get into the Box, a special shelter on the palace's ground floor.

Colón grabbed an AK-47 from the wall rack and prepared to defend himself.

Four men strode purposefully through the dark central hallway as he left the nearly hidden security control center. They, too, were carrying AK-47s, with handguns on their hips.

"What do you know, boss?" his first assistant asked. It was a pleasant greeting they had exchanged daily for the past thirteen years. But tonight, under the circumstances, it took on a darker implication.

Colón shook his head. "I know they're very knowledgeable and well-trained. They came in silent and well-equipped. They knew exactly what they were doing. Like they had blueprints of this place."

"They somehow arranged for this place to be nearly unguarded tonight, didn't they?" the assistant asked.

Colón shrugged. "Looks like it. Yes, it has to be. They set us up. They set up the president."

"Who's 'they,' though?"

"That I don't know."

The five men exchanged worried glances. "But they can't get at the president and the vice president, can they?" one of the guards asked.

Colón shook his head. "They cannot. Of that I'm sure. If they made it to the Box." He grabbed at the walkie-talkie on his belt. "Ramon, come in. Ramon, talk to me."

A strange noise came over the walkie-talkie, and they realized it was the sound of chaos—explosions, gunfire and shouting. They heard Ramon speak.

"They've blown the wall! They're at the entrance to the…!"

"Ramon? We didn't catch that."

"They've blown the wall at the Box!" Ramon shouted through the communicator.

The Box was the secure compartment on the ground floor. It was meant to house the president and his family in case of an attack. Theoretically it would survive anything less than a nearby hit with a nuclear weapon.

"Did the president make it inside?" Colón asked.

There was some kind of a response from Ramon, but the words were lost in an explosion and a scream.

"Ramon?"

The walkie-talkie was silent.

"Ramon, come in!"

There was another burst of noise. "They're gone—all my men! I'm the only one left and they'll get me any second!"

"Did the president and his family get into the Box?" Colón demanded urgently.

"Yes!" Ramon shouted back. "They are safe—"

The word transformed into a scream and a hiss of static, then the walkie-talkie was silent. The five guards had reached the end of the cool, dark hallway and Colón put his hand on the door.

"Wait!" It was one of the guards.

Colón looked at him.

"Ramon is dead. All the guards are dead. We're all that's left."

Colón said nothing.

"If we go, then we go to our deaths. There are too many soldiers out there for us to have any hopes of winning the battle. And they will never get to the president if he is safe in the Box."

"What are you saying?"

"I know what he is saying," Colón's assistant said. "I agree with him. To go and fight these men is suicide and purposeless. We should wait for reinforcements."

"How do we know reinforcements are coming?" Colón demanded.

"The explosions will have been heard," the assistant suggested, but not with great conviction.

"They're all waiting at the assembly. They think the attack will come there," Colón declared. "If we don't fight these men, then no one will."

"To what end?" his assistant demanded.

Colón tried to answer but couldn't find the right words. He

aid, "I go to fight if for no other reason than to uphold my
wn sense of honor."

"Is that enough reason?"

"Yes!"

Colón turned and opened the door and stared down a broad
tairway. There were two men moving in the great ballroom
t the base of the stairs, who turned when they spotted the
novement, drawing their autorifles. Colón dropped into a
rouch and heard the wide double doors behind him, and for
he instant it took him to raise his AK-47 into target acquisi-
ion he didn't know if any or all or none of his guards were
till with him. He triggered the weapon and heard the eruption
f fire from just over his shoulder and the two ate the rounds,
ollapsing on the marble floor.

Another intruder had been hiding in the shadows, and when
e saw his comrades go down he bolted for the door. Colón
tarted down the steps after him and began to fire, but as the
urvivor ran for escape a half dozen of his companions entered
he ballroom and leveled their weapons at Colón and the pal-
ce guards.

His men had been right. This was a suicide run. They had
o hope of surviving. A quick glance over his shoulder
howed him that all four of his guards were still with him.

He ran at the intruders, triggering his AK, and heard the
ootsteps of his men at his heels.

BOLAN SNATCHED an MP-5 from the store behind the seat of
he helicopter and grabbed the pack of spare magazines that
ame with it.

"Whatever air security this place once had, it's inoperative
ow," Grimaldi declared. The JetRanger was over the grounds
f the palace, a dark and ominous complex of buildings below
hem.

"Look there." The pilot moved the searchlight over what
vas clearly a helicopter landing pad on the roof. Three bodies
ay there, clutching unused weapons.

"Let's go in," Bolan said.

"Right."

The JetRanger swept out of the sky and braked to a ha[?] over the landing pad, then descended the final four feet in [?] hurry. Bolan swung open the door as a figure stepped fro[?] the shadows and commenced firing an automatic rifle at th[?] bird. Bolan heard the impact of the rounds on the steel an[?] glass inches from his shoulder and triggered the MP-5 at th[?] source, sending a deadly torrent of 9 mm rounds into the shad[?] ows. The autofire stopped, and a man sprawled on his face i[?] the pale moonlight.

Bolan jogged to the figure and flipped it over, causing th[?] man to issue a grunt of pain. He had a punctured lung an[?] didn't have long to live.

"How many?" Bolan demanded.

The dying man grimaced. "Fuck you." he said, his accer[?] East Coast U.S. He was one of Fagen's mercenaries. He stare[?] at the sky, and his features froze in death.

19

They found an entrance to the building and entered together, Bolan aiming high, Grimaldi aiming his Uzi low.

They found empty rooms and a set of wide, sweeping stairs that went down in a single flight into a huge ballroom or reception room—a stairway worthy of a palace. Halfway down the steps, gleaming in the harsh blare of the emergency lighting system, was a splash of blood. The sticky trail led to the bottom, where two guards lay, head shot and battered by their crashing descent.

The huge room was silent.

"I'm beginning to think we're too late," Grimaldi said.

"Yeah. Maybe."

Another dead guard lay at a pair of wide-open double doors, leading into a hallway at least a hundred feet long and lit by a single emergency light.

The Cuban palace was still as death.

Bolan would have a hard time feeling sorrow for the death of the totalitarian president or his brother, but they were better than a new, strong, orthodox Communist dictator. Resnikoff had to be removed. That was the only solution.

The Executioner was beginning to regret bringing Grimaldi. While there was no warrior he would rather have fighting at his side, this might very well turn into a suicide battle with no survivors on either side. Bolan was willing to make that sacrifice. If this was his final battle, if he wasn't fated to live to see the next morning, that was fine with him. He hated to

bring one of his true friends into such a battle. He had no wish
to doom Grimaldi.

But he knew Grimaldi was more than ready to die at his
side if that was what this night's battle called for.

Death might very well be on the agenda, but it would be a
warrior's death, hard-fought.

A figure in black stepped out of the darkness, snarling, aiming one of those shining new AK-74 autorifles. The Executioner didn't know who he was, didn't care who he was. The
warrior stepped into the figure and triggered a burst that blew
the attacker onto his back on the marble floor. As the Stony
Man pair raced forward, a muffled blast rocked the palace like
an earthquake.

"HOW MUCH LONGER?" Resnikoff shouted.

"Five minutes!" called back the Russian at the helm of the
drill.

"Good!" He looked around nervously. He was expecting a
horde of Cuban soldiers to appear at any minute, but that was
only his paranoia. The palace was virtually abandoned. The
guards were extinct or in hiding.

Everything was going ahead as planned. Even the loss of
the Colombians hadn't been a major obstacle. The palace had
been as easy to break into as a nursery school.

"Look what we found!" one of the Americans shouted,
herding a bent, broken-looking man. "Chief of palace
security!"

Resnikoff laughed and grabbed the man by the collar. His
eyes had been pounded until they swelled shut, but he turned
as if to look at Resnikoff.

"You should have played along. You might have kept your
job," Resnikoff said evenly. "I'll be in need of my own chief
of palace security. On second thought, I wouldn't have hired
you, anyway. You obviously aren't effective in the position."

"You'll never get at the president."

Resnikoff held Colón's head and clawed one swollen eye
open. "Think again, friend. We'll get at your precious presi-

lent in just a few minutes. And in just a few minutes he will
be dead.''

BOLAN AND GRIMALDI found themselves on the palace
grounds and circled in the direction of the explosion until they
reached a cavernlike opening blown in the wall. They fell back
as the guards opened fire with their Kalashnikovs.

"They landed something big and heavy here—look at the
chute," Grimaldi said, indicating a massive expanse of silk
that was caught in one of the palace trees.

"Then they blew a new entrance to get it inside," Bolan
said, nodding at the gaping opening. "Let's go find out what
it is and what they're doing with it."

He stepped around the corner triggering the MP-5, cutting
down one of the guards. The other saved himself by leaping
behind the wall. He appeared again long enough to trigger a
burst of autofire, but Bolan fired simultaneously. The guard's
weapon clattered to the ground and he fell face-forward, then
stopped moving.

They crept to the wall and peered down another hallway,
descending at an angle. Here the wall coverings had been torn
off to reveal what looked like a gigantic vault door. A piece
of heavy machinery on treads was before the door, assaulting
it with what appeared to be a mining drill. The three-foot-long
shaft was inches thick and had already penetrated several
inches into the vault door.

"Looks like the president has a secret hiding place in case
of such an emergency," Grimaldi observed.

"Looks like the Russians not only knew about it, they knew
how to break into it," Bolan said.

The men marching up the incline didn't see the blacksuited
warriors until they cut loose with their weapons. Two went
down as the rest dived for cover, and Bolan stepped into the
open to get a clear shot at the drill operator. He unloaded
another half-dozen rounds into the distant piece of machinery.
The whine of the drill engine suddenly died, and the operator
slumped to the side and collapsed from the equipment.

Bolan retreated behind the wall with his partner, satisfied he had slowed the operation substantially. An errant sound, maybe just warrior's instinct, motivated him to look up and he spotted movement on the roof above them.

Two faces appeared at the edge of the roof, and Bolan swept the submachine gun at them, firing a steady stream. An AK-74 fell from the roof, hitting the ground with a clatter. One of the faces appeared again and fired wildly at them, slumping under the onslaught of sustained fire from H & K and Uzi.

"Let's get inside," Bolan suggested as he slammed another magazine into the MP-5, then stepped into the open, firing a steady stream, sweeping the hallway in front of him. Grimaldi was at his side, the Uzi chattering and slapping down two gunmen attempting to approach from the near wall. They found themselves in another hallway and listened to the rattle of gunfire pepper the emptiness of their former positions.

Bolan had spotted a tall figure dragging the dead drill operator off the machine. He peered around the corner long enough to see him scrambling to get inside the drill cage himself. He pulled back, gave the new operator time to get in place, then leveled the MP-5 around the corner and rattled off several rounds that left gaping red holes in his back.

RESNIKOFF SHOUTED in rage when he watched the second drill operator killed in his seat.

"Rush them. It's only two men. What are you waiting for?"

"All right!" Fagen shouted, and gestured to his men to spread out in formation, then they advanced up the inclined floor to the corner. Several of them jumped around the corner simultaneously, triggering blasts and holding up suddenly.

"They're gone," Fagen shouted back to Resnikoff.

Then there was a rattle of gunfire, and Fagen was stepping backward rapidly, his gun falling and his arms flapping uselessly like a scarecrow's. He dropped to the ground in a mess of his own blood. Three more collapsed suddenly, and the rest of the mercenaries were falling back.

"They're in hiding. We didn't even see them," one man shouted.

"Get in position," Resnikoff roared to his Russian soldiers. "You!" he yelled at the mercenaries. "Take them down."

BOLAN STEPPED OUT of the double-wide doorway into the pitch-black room that had served as cover. He grabbed at one of the bodies and hoisted it onto its back, snatching up the grenades on the corpse's belt. He pulled the pins on all three and ran to the corner, lobbing the bombs down the incline and retreating for cover. The blast overwhelmed the hall, and a huge cloud of debris and dust billowed out the opening, into the night. Bolan was already moving into the dust, bending over another of the dead mercenaries and quickly relieving him of his grenades. The Executioner didn't bother figuring out what type they were before he yanked their pins and sent them into the chaos at the end of the hall. He dived out the gaping hole in the wall, landing face-first on the grass, and felt the earth shake as the three blasts shook the palace and the grounds, then jumped to his feet, leveling the MP-5.

At least one of the grenades had been a smoker, and the hall filled with thick, black clouds. Bolan heard someone staggering through the rubble ahead of him and he grabbed the man, buried the MP-5 in his gut and triggered briefly. The man fell into the wall, then to his knees, and collapsed on the ground.

Another man staggered out of the clouds and rammed into Bolan, but the soldier sidestepped the attack and sent the man slamming onto his back.

The figure barreled to his feet and swung wildly with his fists, and Bolan saw the man was blinded—his face was blackened and his eyes were burned shut.

Bolan recognized him anyway.

"Here I am, Resnikoff."

The Russian general charged Bolan, who stepped out of the way and allowed the blind man to trip over the rubble where the wall was blasted open.

Another Russian charged through the smoke and swung an AK-74 at the warrior. Bolan avoided the swing and triggered the MP-5, and the Russian collapsed.

The smoke was clearing and the air became less opaque.

Resnikoff stood but failed to keep his balance and fell onto his hands and knees. He had broken a burned crust of skin over his left eye, and blood was pouring down his face. He wiped it from his mouth with his sleeve.

"Tell me who you are," Resnikoff said.

"Just a man, General."

"Not any longer."

Resnikoff rose up with an AK-74 in his hands and fired it.

Bolan watched the 5.45 mm hollowpoints slash into the blackened walls and the smoking floor. Resnikoff was swinging in Bolan's direction, trying to sweep the area, but Bolan raised the muzzle of the MP-5, fired and drilled a burst into Resnikoff's head, ending his quest for a new revolution.

Another man staggered in Bolan's direction and stopped suddenly when a rattle of Uzi fire stitched him up the back and flung him on his face. Grimaldi appeared with the smoking subgun. "Maybe we should make our exit before the Cubans get their Strategic Air Command back on-line."

There were mercenaries and Russians alive yet in the mess. Bolan would let the Cubans sort them out.

He glanced back at the vaultlike door, behind which the president and vice president of Cuba hid, perhaps terrified that they were about to be executed. The grenade blasts had only dented the door slightly.

"I'd say the president got what he paid for in that door," Grimaldi said.

EPILOGUE

"The government of Cuba denies they've had any breach in national security," Brognola said. "A few high-ranking types have vanished, but they aren't saying who."

"It doesn't matter now," Bolan replied. He and Grimaldi were eating a room-service meal in a hotel in Key West. Bolan had slept a luxurious eight hours to make up for several days of almost no sleep.

"Yeah, the threat is over," the big Fed said, his voice sounding tired over the hotel-room phone speaker. "This threat. For now. Where did you refuel the JetRanger, by the way?"

"Cárdenas," Grimaldi replied. "When we got there it was more or less abandoned. I think everybody was headed to Havana. Anyway, nobody protested. Does this mean Striker and I can take a few days R and R on the beach?"

"That's up to Striker," Brognola said, and made his goodbyes.

Bolan said nothing but pulled out the scarred leather book from his shirt pocket and opened it to a page of scrawled notes. At the end of the page was the name *Manny Quinones*.

Grimaldi looked at it and nodded.

"I take it this means no R and R?"

Bolan nodded. No time for rest.

Iran ups the ante in Bosnia with new weapons of terror....

STONY MAN™ 37

TRIPLE STRIKE

A kidnapped U.S. advisor and a downed recon plane pilot are held in a stronghold in Muslim Bosnia, where Iranian forces have joined with their Bosnian brothers to eradicate the unbelievers.

The President and Stony Man must use their individual powers of influence to bring the agents of doom to justice–if there's still time....

Available in November 1998 at your favorite retail outlet.

It's blitzkreig time as new and improved Nazis invade Europe!

THE

Destroyer™

#113 The Empire Dreams
The Fatherland Files Book II

Created by
WARREN MURPHY
and RICHARD SAPIR

Vacationing in London, Dr. Harold Smith feels a strange déjà vu as World War II planes bomb the city and skinheads roam the streets.

A rogue Nazi with a new blueprint for world domination becomes Remo's target as the world gets stranger by the minute.

This is the second in The Fatherland Files, a miniseries based on a secret fascist organization's attempts to regain the glory of the Third Reich.

Available in November at your favorite retail outlet.

In the badlands, there is only survival....

JAMES AXLER

DEATHLANDS®

Crucible of Time

A connection to his past awaits Ryan Cawdor as the group takes a mat-trans jump to the remnants of California. Brother Joshua Wolfe is the leader of the Children of the Rock—a cult that has left a trail of barbarism and hate across the ravaged California countryside. Far from welcoming the group with open arms, the cult forces them into a deadly battle-ritual— which is only their first taste of combat....

James Axler

OUTLANDERS™

ICEBLOOD

Kane and his companions race to find a piece of the Chintamanti Stone, which they believe to have power over the collective mind of the evil Archons. Their journey sees them foiled by a Russian mystic named Zakat in Manhattan, and there is another dangerous encounter waiting for them in the Kun Lun mountains of China.

One man's quest for power unleashes a cataclysm in America's wastelands.